# Remembering the Titanic

# DIANE HOH

SCHOLASTIC INC.
New York Toronto London Auckland Sydney

ISBN 0-590-87585-X

Copyright © 1998 by Diane Hoh.
All rights reserved. Published by Scholastic Inc.
SCHOLASTIC and logos are trademarks and/or registered trademarks of Scholastic Inc.

12 11 10 9 8 7 6 5 4 3 2 1          8 9/9 0 1 2 3/0

Printed in the U.S.A.

First Scholastic printing, August 1998

# Prologue

The North Atlantic Ocean, where the icebergs are, is still, a navy blue satin blanket covering the earth for endless miles. Barely a ripple breaks the surface, and then only in the wake of a ship.

But that stillness is deceptive. A dark, painful history lies beneath that placid water. Only those who were part of that history know just how painful.

There are secrets lying deep below the ocean's surface. Unheard ... unseen ...

But never forgotten.

# Chapter 1

Elizabeth Farr was cold. And she was angry. She was angry with her mother for insisting that Elizabeth wear one of the new, lightweight spring suits, ordered from their dressmaker. It was pretty enough, the color a deep shade of rose, and of course it was the latest fashion, with its hobbled skirt and narrow waistline. The wide-brimmed, veiled hat matched perfectly. Nola would never settle for anything less. She would have fired Madame Claude-Pierre in a second if the woman failed to keep up with the latest designs from Paris. As if to compensate for a full year of wearing somber black mourning apparel, Nola had ordered enough spring fashions to fill every wardrobe in the house to overflowing.

Elizabeth cared little about fashion now. What seemed far more important was warming the ever-present, painful chill in her bones. She missed the heavy woolens she'd worn all winter, although they hadn't helped much, either. It was April again, a full year from that terrifying night out on the cold, black sea. Shivering with both fear and cold, Elizabeth had watched in horrified disbelief from her lifeboat as the great ship *Titanic* raised upright in the ocean, pointing toward the sky like an arrow, before breaking in two and sinking forever. To Elizabeth, it still seemed like yesterday. The long, painful vigil in the lifeboat, her limbs and face so cold she could scarcely feel them, could have taken place the night before, so clear were those hours in her mind. Now, try though she would, she could not banish the constant chill in her bones. Nor could she silence the remembered screams of victims as they flailed helplessly in the frigid ocean, realizing, in those agonizing last moments, that no one was coming to their rescue. No one.

One lifeboat . . . only one . . . had searched for survivors. But by then, it was much too late.

Her mother and Max, the two people she loved most in the world, seemed to have recovered better than she had. How, she wondered, had Max put the tragedy so easily behind him? That night had been far worse for him. She'd been safe in a lifeboat while he, flung into the ocean when the ship finally slid beneath the surface, struggled in the dark, numbing water.

Yet even at Christmastime, in the penetrating cold, and when the threat of snow was in the air, Max had arrived at the Farrs' Murray Hill mansion wearing only an overcoat. No scarf, no hat, no gloves. Elizabeth envied that, too. How did he shrug off the cold when she, even in April, shivered with it?

"It's been eight months, Elizabeth," he had said on Christmas Eve after presenting her with a beautiful gold locket and the sheet music for a new song she liked, "and you're still cold all the time. Maybe you should see a doctor."

A doctor? She had looked at him skeptically. How could a doctor help?

She had not gone to a doctor. She had simply piled on more clothing. On evenings when her mother wasn't dragging her to yet another boring dinner or concert or play, she lay on the pink brocade chaise lounge in her room with one woolen lap robe wrapped around her chest and shoulders, another tucked around her legs while she read for the third time Gene Stratton Porter's *Girl of the Limberlost*. And always, always, there was a fire blazing in her fireplace.

None of it helped. Spring was in the air on this day in April when so many people had gathered at the Seamen's Church Institute in New York City for the dedication of the *Titanic* Memorial Lighthouse. Wrapping her arms around her chest in an effort to keep warm, she tried to focus her attention on the ceremony. Her mother was at her side, Max in the crowd somewhere, sketching. The mood was grim. Some present were openly crying, their anguish still raw. Others wore bleak expressions as they recalled receiving the news of a loved one's death on the great, "unsinkable" ship.

Elizabeth had often thought how painful it must have been for the relatives and friends waiting on shore. Doubly painful because the initial newspaper reports falsely stated that all on board had been rescued. On the contrary, fifteen hundred people had died when the ship sank. How bitter that later news must have been for those who had been rejoicing, believing their loved ones were safe.

Glancing around to see where Max might be, she noticed with interest a few young working women. She envied them their independence. Along with the typical secretary's uniform of serge skirt, white shirtwaist, and inexpensive, tailored jacket, some wore the yellow flowers of the suffragette movement. Elizabeth hoped her mother didn't see the flowers. She was sure to comment. Nola despised the efforts of women to secure the vote, hated their highly publicized marches through the city, their "strident voices" raised "all across the country." With no interest of her own in politics, she failed to understand the needs of other women to have more of a say in such matters.

When she located Max, a rush of warmth flooded Elizabeth, as it always did when she looked at him. Sketch pad in hand, his head was down as he concentrated furiously. His light brown hair needed cutting, as always, though that didn't take away from his attractiveness. What she loved most about him were his eyes, a deep blue. Navy blue when he was feeling most intense or excited.

Still, as much as Elizabeth loved Max, she felt strongly that he shouldn't be sketching the faces, and she decided to say so. Telling her mother she'd be right back, she hurried over to him. He smiled when he saw her, but continued to draw.

"I wish you wouldn't do that," Elizabeth said, touching his arm.

He raised his head then, a look of surprise on his lean, handsome face. "Do what?"

"Sketch people. Not now, not here. They're grieving, Max. You're invading their privacy."

He frowned. "They don't even know I'm doing it."

"It's still an intrusion." She pointed toward the brown-suited men armed with cameras moving through the crowd. "Isn't it bad enough that the press has arrived? We're here to remember the loved ones we lost a year ago, and it's wrong to take advantage of that. Our privacy should be respected."

"Privacy? Elizabeth, this is a public place."

"I don't care. Please, Max. Not now." She was disappointed in him. It wasn't like Max to take advantage of the pain of others. He was kinder and more sensitive than that. What had gotten into him?

Max didn't put his sketch pad away. But he said, "I'll sketch the Lighthouse memorial instead," and began to do just that.

Elizabeth had to admit this new memorial was intriguing. The Lighthouse mounted on the institute's roof was topped with a black ball that would drop each afternoon at one P.M. (though Elizabeth puzzled over why they had picked that specific hour since the ship itself had sunk in the wee hours of the morning). A light had been put inside the ball. It was green, the color of hope. It all seemed more impressive than a simple bronze plaque.

Although she was still shivering slightly, Elizabeth concentrated on the words being spoken in memory of the father she still missed fiercely and in memory of the fifteen hundred other people who had perished in the disaster.

Far from where Elizabeth stood, on the fringes of the crowd, Katie Hanrahan fidgeted restlessly. Though she, too, had spent that long, frightening night in a lifeboat, she was not plagued by an incessant chill as Elizabeth was. Frequent nightmares and a fear of dark, enclosed spaces were her legacies. The nights were the worst. During the daytime hours she was usually busy enough to keep from thinking about the ill-fated journey from her home in Ireland. There were household chores in her aunt's roominghouse, and trips into Manhattan for auditions and meetings with theatrical agents in hopes of establishing a singing career. That career, though it had yet to get off the ground, had been her goal in traveling to America. Her days were very busy.

But she had no control over the dark dreams that stalked her sleep. She woke from them in a state of panic, drenched in a clammy sweat, convinced that she was still trapped in the belly of the sinking *Titanic*.

Still, she could handle the nightmares. A cup of warm milk, a chapter or two read in a favorite book, and sleep would return.

What was harder to handle was Paddy's stubborn refusal to attend a single memorial for victims of the *Titanic*. She needed him with her during these painful ceremonies. Did he not miss his brother Brian, who hadn't been as lucky as they? Where was his respect for his older sibling? If it hadn't been for Brian, neither one of them would have made it to America. It was Brian her da trusted, not his younger brother. Everyone in Ballyford liked Paddy well enough, but that didn't mean they trusted him with their daughters. On the contrary, he had left behind a string of broken hearts.

Katie smiled, thinking how determined she had been not to join that sad group, in spite of Paddy's charm and good looks. But those days on the *Titanic* ... the happy days before the shocking end to the journey ... had changed all that. To her astonishment, she had discovered a side to Paddy that she'd never known existed ... a sensitive, caring side that had nearly kept him from leaving his brother on the sinking ship. If Brian hadn't insisted that Paddy might be needed to help out in the lifeboats, both brothers would have perished.

Katie sighed. Why wasn't Paddy here, at her side at this dedication ceremony, instead of her aunt Lottie? Lottie hadn't lost a loved one in the disaster. She had accompanied her niece only because she disapproved of Katie traveling from Brooklyn alone and because she, a soft-hearted woman, felt deeply about the tragedy. Surely Paddy should feel the same. But he didn't seem to.

"I don't see the point to all of these ceremonies and all this fuss," he had said. "What good does it do? We need to be gettin' on with our lives here in America, not belaborin' the past. 'Tis over and done with, and best forgotten."

Forgotten? Katie had been shocked and furious. How could it be forgotten? Hadn't it been the worst night of their lives? She'd forget her own name before she'd forget a single moment of that night.

As if the nightmares weren't bad enough, she could no longer bear to be in small, enclosed spaces. Elevators in the city were an endurance test for her. If it was at all possible to take a flight of stairs instead, she did so, though her aunt insisted staircases were not safe and Katie should never use them. "You don't know who might be lurking in a stairwell," she would say. But to Katie, even an enclosed stairwell was not as terrifying as the four walls of an elevator. Besides, she had argued, why couldn't someone be "lurking" in an elevator as well?

She knew why the closed-in feeling haunted her. 'Twas a reminder of the suffocating moments she had spent in the depths of the ship, after the *Titanic* struck the iceberg, and she tried to find her way up from the steerage lower deck to the top of the ship where the lifeboats were stationed. Accompanied by two small children whose governess had abandoned them, she had navigated the puzzling twists and turns of the narrow subterranean corridors in vain, trying to find a way to escape the water rushing into the ship at an alarming rate. The passageways were so narrow, the corridor so deep in the bowels of the ship, she had felt as if she were suffocating. Panic had risen within her steadily.

If Paddy hadn't found them. . . .

But he had. He had taken them up top, where they had eventually gotten into one of the few remaining lifeboats. Then there had been that terrifying moment when Paddy had been required to stay behind, as Katie climbed into the lifeboat. Only women and children were allowed to board. If, at the last moment, he hadn't been ordered to help crew the lifeboat, she'd have lost him, too. Bad enough to lose one Kelleher, let alone the Kelleher she loved so deeply. She had loved Brian, too, but not in the same way. Her passion for Paddy was the deepest, truest feeling she had ever known. And she missed him now just as passionately, so busy was he with his new, exciting life. He had had better luck in America with his dreams than she with hers.

"What time are ye meetin' with that agent?" her aunt Lottie asked loudly. "His Nibs gets testy when his dinner isn't ready on time. You know that as well as me."

Katie nodded. Her uncle had a temper, and he liked things to be just so. Still, he'd been good to her, taking her in and giving her a home. "We've plenty of time. But you needn't come with me. I can get there on me own."

Her aunt shook her head. "You'll not be wanderin' around the city alone. What would your uncle say, was I to let you do that? I'll come. I'm just sayin', we can't be hangin' around that office all day, that's all I'm sayin'."

"I know." Katie fell silent, lost in unhappy thought. Her aunt was fretting for nothing. When had she ever been in an agent's office for more than a few minutes? She was always hurt and puzzled by how hastily she was shown the door. She was certain it wasn't her attire that was the cause. The ruffled, bright pink dress she'd had Lottie make for her was the prettiest dress she'd ever owned. Katie had seen it in a magazine and thought it just right for impressing agents. Another magazine article had showed her how to arrange her hair in a fancy 'do. She had even persuaded her aunt that if she was going to succeed, she simply had to wear makeup. So she was certain it couldn't be her appearance that led agents to interrupt her in mid-refrain while she was belting out the latest songs just as she'd heard them on John Donnelly's phonograph. It had to be something else that led them to mutter an insincere, "Very nice. We'll call you," and rush her to the door.

Of course they never called. Her aunt and

uncle had a telephone. Katie was always very careful to write the number down clearly and legibly, but to no avail. Not so much as one agent had called on the telephone to say they wished to further Katie Hanrahan's singing career.

But she wasn't giving up. If only this new agent would be pleased with her voice. . . .

And if only Paddy were here to meet the agent with her. As she had gone with him to meet his publisher, Edmund Tyree. She'd been nervous about meeting such an important man, but Paddy had insisted, saying he needed her with him. Well, now she needed him. But he wasn't here. And truth to tell, she didn't know exactly where he was. She knew only, as she did so often now, that he wasn't with her.

Glancing around as if he might be lurking somewhere in the crowd, Katie gasped when she glimpsed a young man with a sketch pad in his hand. She blinked in surprise, and peered more closely. Did she not recognize him as a passenger on board the *Titanic*? A very special passenger, at that. She would never forget him. The young man had risked his own life to deposit the two young charges in her care into a lifeboat. He had had to stand outside the ship's rail to reach, and had nearly fallen into the sea in the process. The pretty girl standing with him had called him "Max," and was clearly very fond of him. This "Max" had lived? He had survived and returned to New York safely?

Katie's heart flooded with warmth. How wonderful for both of them! The saints be praised!

She glanced around again, this time for some sign of his companion on the *Titanic*. A very pretty first-class passenger, she'd had great difficulty leaving him behind as she and her mother boarded a lifeboat. Katie had felt sorry for her, watching her being torn from both her father, a handsome man with kind eyes, and the young man she clearly loved.

Were the pretty girl from the ship and this Max still in love, as they'd seemed to be on the ship? Perhaps not, since they were not together today. Might they have discovered, once on shore, that the closeness they'd shared on the *Titanic* was gone, as if it had tumbled into the sea and disappeared along with the fine china, the pianos, the luggage, and the jewelry lost forever to the deep, dark water?

Ever the romantic, Katie hoped that hadn't happened. They had seemed to be so much in love. And they were so fortunate that the young man was still alive, for her own lifeboat had been one of the last to leave and he hadn't been in it. How had he survived the sea?

She spied the girl then. Dressed in a smart-looking suit the color of a summer rose, she was standing next to the beautiful woman from the ship. Her mother. No father, sad to say. He had not been, then, as lucky as the young man. The girl looked thinner, and she was shivering visibly, her arms around her chest, as if to keep warm. Quiet tears ran down her cheeks.

Katie felt a sharp flash of annoyance at the artist. Was he too busy with his drawing to put a comforting arm around the girl's shoulders? She had been forced to leave her father behind on the sinking ship, and must have a broken heart. Clucking her tongue in disgust, Katie turned away. What earthly good did it do to have a fellow if he wasn't around when you needed him? Might as well get yourself a tabby cat. They'd sit on your lap for hours if you wanted and all they asked in return was a nice dish of milk now and again.

"We'd best leave now," she told her aunt. "The speeches could go on for quite a while. I don't want to be late to the agent."

As they departed the memorial ceremony, she glanced back once more over her shoulder. The young man from the ship was still sketching. And the girl, looking very much alone in spite of her mother standing alongside her, was still shivering.

# Chapter 2

When Elizabeth and her mother had been chauffeured away to yet another appointment with the dressmaker, Max stayed behind to put the finishing touches on his sketch of the new memorial. He hadn't planned to draw it. It was unnecessary. Every newspaper in the world would carry at least one picture of it in tomorrow's issue. Why create yet another?

But Elizabeth's request had changed his mind. He had to draw something and if it wasn't to be faces, it had to be the memorial. Besides, the drawing would fit in nicely with the new paintings scattered all over his apartment. Elizabeth hadn't seen them yet. Her mother had strong opinions about a young woman visiting a young man's apartment. He had invited Mrs. Farr, too, once or twice, knowing how difficult it was for Elizabeth to get away. But he hadn't really expected the woman to appear on his doorstep. Though she was a born-and-raised New Yorker, he suspected that Greenwich Village was far more foreign to her than Paris and London, which she had visited many times.

The avenue on which he lived wasn't bad. Better than some. It was neat and clean, and boasted a few moderately sized trees here and there. His parents refused to support him financially until he "came to his senses" and joined the family's business. But the death this past winter of his grandmother, whom he still missed, had provided him with a generous trust fund. He used the money sparingly, preferring to make his own way for the most part. Still, it had allowed him to rent a decent apartment in a fairly safe neighborhood, where no gangs of young thugs roamed, looking to pick a pocket or two.

Max sighed as he stepped across a large puddle, a souvenir of the previous night's spring rain. He saw so little of Elizabeth now. Things were not at all as they'd expected . . . as *he'd* expected . . . when they had first discovered their feelings for each other while crossing on the *Titanic*. Remembering their first encounter, he laughed softly to himself. While Elizabeth and her family had boarded the huge luxury ship in Southampton, he had not embarked until Cherbourg. He had fallen in love with France, but after spending a full year there, he knew it was time to go home and begin forging his own art career. When he boarded the ship, he had needed a haircut, had carried his own luggage on board, and his jacket, he had to admit, could have used the ministrations of a good tailor. So he shouldn't have been surprised when Elizabeth mistook him for a steerage passenger and tried, kindly enough, to direct him to the third-class facilities. He hadn't corrected her, hadn't even spoken, not wanting to embarrass her. So she had assumed he was French and spoke no English.

Remembering, Max laughed aloud, attracting curious looks from people passing on the street. She had looked so shocked later that day when she discovered him sitting in the first-class dining room. *He's* not supposed to be here, said the expression on her face. She'd been even more shocked a moment later when her own father, Martin Farr, introduced Max as the son of family friends . . . in other words, belonging to the same social class as Elizabeth. Her cheeks had turned as red as an ocean sunset, and she'd clearly been furious. Max hadn't been sure whom she was angrier with . . . him, her father . . . or herself, for making such an embarrassing mistake.

Whatever her first impression had been, his had been of a lovely but spoiled, headstrong girl who seemed to be forever storming out of one of the ship's many rooms at one point or another. When he learned how diligently she was fighting to escape a debut she didn't want and a marriage she wanted even less, to a very proper but, she said, "dull as dishwater" banker, he changed his mind. She *was*, of course, spoiled. He hadn't been wrong about that. Most young women in her situation were. But there was more to Elizabeth than he'd first thought. Her feelings were passionate, her opinions equally so, her ambition fierce. At least, it had seemed so then. She had wanted desperately to go to college, earn a degree, "*do* something with my life," she had cried as she stood with Max at the *Titanic*'s rail, watching the flat, black satin sea glide by. Her parents, however, were insisting that she make the planned debut and then marry Alan Reed, who sounded to Max like an unsuitable mate for a young woman with Elizabeth's fire. It was a stormy crossing for the Farr family.

Max frowned. That fire he'd seen in Elizabeth . . . if it wasn't gone, it had at least been dampened. She spent most of her time now being the devoted daughter, attending concerts and plays and dinners, always in her mother's company. If he complained, as he had more than once, that he saw too little of her, she would put her hand on his arm, look into his eyes, and say, "But Max, I promised my father!"

That promise, on board the ship... Max wished fervently Martin had never asked it of Elizabeth. Would he really want his daughter living the staid life of a society matron? She was only eighteen. On the ship, she had complained often about the banality of her mother's life. She had spoken heatedly of how she would hate such a life, how she would *never* follow Nola's example. How could she stand it now? And with so little complaint.

Max understood why she was doing it. Her father's last request before Elizabeth and her mother left the ship without him had been to "take care of your mother." She had taken that request seriously and was doing everything in her power to fulfill it. She had loved her father very much. Small wonder that his death had changed her, perhaps forever.

Elizabeth, too, had come close to dying. Had the rescue ship *Carpathia* not come along when it did, no one would have survived. Instead of fifteen hundred deaths, there would have been closer to twenty-five hundred.

There were times when she tried to talk about that night. But he couldn't. He didn't know how. At least, he didn't know how to talk about it in a way that would make Elizabeth feel better, restore her to her former self, and push her out of the Farr mansion and into a life of her own.

A life which would, of course, include Max Whittaker, in a way that it now did not. With Nola monopolizing Elizabeth's time, Max had been forced to create a social life of his own, make new friends, most aspiring artists like himself. For a while, he'd been incredibly busy. Coming so precariously close to death had given him a new taste for living. He slept very little those first few months after the rescue, intent on filling every minute with new and interesting things. He was studying with a well-known painter and when he wasn't studying or working on his own paintings, he was exploring every inch of New York City, finding it even more fascinating than he had before. He sought out new restaurants, new plays, explored new buildings as they sprang up, hung out in Tin Pan Alley long enough to hear the latest songs ... there never seemed to be enough time to gulp in as much life as he needed to. Elizabeth almost never came with him. She was too busy accompanying her mother, usually on shopping trips.

Eventually, he had tired of such a hectic life. Now his goal was to fill the apartment with new canvasses. An idea had come to him, and his hands burned with the need to paint. So paint he did . . . morning, noon, or night, good light, bad light, it made no difference. Nothing else seemed as important.

But he still missed Elizabeth and would rather have spent time with her than with anyone else. If she could find a way to free herself from the prison of her father's promise. . . .

"Hey, Max!" An elbow jabbed Max in the ribs. "What are you up to?"

Max winced at the blow. Never heavy, he had lost weight recently from a combination of hard work and little attention to regular meals. "Watch it, Bledsoe. You don't know your own strength."

Short, blond Norman Bledsoe shrugged. In an attempt to age his round, babyish face, he was striving to grow a beard. The fair hair barely covered his chin, and the effect, rather than maturing him, gave him a slight air of disrepute, though his gray pants and black overcoat were clean and neat enough. Without an invitation, he fell into step beside Max. "Are you ready to let us see your new work? We're getting impatient, Max. Anne and Gregory are suspicious. They think you're not working at all, that you're just pretending to. You need to prove them wrong. Besides, you're the only one with enough room in your place for a get-together, and we haven't had one there in ages. I'm tired of having to fold myself up like an accordion just to fit in everyone else's hovels."

Max shrugged. They rounded the corner into his avenue. As always, he felt a surge of satisfaction that this was *his* home he was returning to, not his parents'. Instead of the enormous four-story brick house in which he had been raised, he was advancing toward a trio of small, but perfectly adequate rooms of his own. He and Anne Morrison, Bledsoe's girlfriend, were the only two in their group who possessed more than one tiny, dismal room. But Anne's was in a terrible neighborhood, under the elevated trains.

"So?" Norman pressed. "When can I tell the others you're ready for the unveiling of your new work?"

"I'll have a get-together when I'm ready to show my work. At my place. Maybe I can even talk Elizabeth's mother into letting her come. Just the one time. You'll have to wait until then."

The need to return to his painting overtook him then. Impatient and anxious, he quickened his steps.

Norman followed suit, but at the same time, he let out a grunt of disbelief. "Elizabeth's mother won't let her come, Max, you know that. Not with a bunch of down-and-out aspiring artists hanging out at your place. But the rest of us will be there. How soon, do you think?"

"How do I know when I'll be ready? You can't put a timetable on art, Bledsoe." They had reached Max's building. His mind already back in his apartment with his canvasses, he waved, ran up the steps, and disappeared inside.

Norman watched him go, shaking his head sadly. To a passing stranger in a tweed overcoat, he said, "You'd think a best friend would want to spend time with you, wouldn't you?"

The stranger, shaking his own head, hurried away.

On the other side of the city, a tall, dark-haired, handsome young man awkwardly holding a delicate porcelain cup in one hand while shaking the hand of an older gentleman with the other, found himself wishing he had skipped this particular event. I should have spent the afternoon with Katie, Paddy Kelleher was thinking even as he gifted the older man, a well-known literary agent, with the smile that had broken so many female hearts back in County Cork, Ireland. He used the smile more often these days to charm the countless publishers, literary agents, established writers, and newspaper columnists paraded before him by Edmund Tyree.

Paddy was grateful to Edmund. The publisher, a kind, warm-hearted man very much like Paddy's own grandad back in Ballyford, had taken notice of the single article Paddy had sold to a magazine six months after his arrival in America. Paddy had titled it, "Surviving the Sea." It was a first-person account of the sinking of the *Titanic*. The magazine's editor had changed the title to "Surviving the *Titanic*," saying that would catch the attention of more readers since the subject was still on everyone's lips six months after the tragedy. Then he had bought and published the article.

Paddy didn't care about the title change. The editor probably knew best. Paddy hadn't used the ship's name because the subject wasn't on *his* lips. He had a difficult time even *saying* the word "*Titanic*." He couldn't talk about it.

He'd been able to at first. He'd talked about the sinking of the great ship like everyone else, mostly to Katie's aunt and uncle, who had listened with wide, horrified eyes.

But then somewhere along the way it came to him, that while he was walking the streets of Manhattan, New York, America, while he was being given the red carpet treatment by Edmund Tyree, who had read his article and now wanted Paddy to write a full-length book about the tragedy, while he was being chauffeured here and there in Edmund's grand Pierce-Arrow automobile, his brother Brian was dead.

While Paddy was attending parties and dinners and meetings, and resting as comfortable as a hen in a nest in the fine apartment Edmund had found for him and was paying the outlandish rent on, while Paddy Kelleher was doing these grand things . . . his older brother Brian was lying, stone-cold, at the bottom of the black Atlantic Ocean. Hadn't even been found to be given a decent church funeral and burial.

The very thought of it, when it hit him as if someone had socked him in the chest, made Paddy sick, sick as a dog. He shook. Nausea hit him in wave upon wave. His vision blurred, and icy chills passed up and down his spine. These things refused to pass until, with great effort, he banished all thought of Brian and the great ship *Titanic* and the North Atlantic Ocean from his mind. But he knew if he allowed the thoughts to return, the illness would as well.

No one knew. Not even Katie.

From that moment on, it was as if he'd been stricken mute about the tragedy. He was afraid to say a word about that long, terrible night, and that was the truth of it. After a while, he even became frightened of writing about it, though he had not yet shared this news with Edmund, or Belle, Edmund's niece, who was tutoring Paddy in grammar and spelling. They still thought he was trying. In a way, he was. But it wasn't doing any good.

Katie knew none of this. And his silence about the horror they'd shared was coming between them, a solid stone wall building up higher and higher. She wanted to talk about that night. Needed to, he guessed. Knowing her as he did, he was certain she was fairly bursting with the need to talk about it. He was just as certain that the person she needed most to talk about it with was himself, him being the one who'd borne most of that long, terrible night right alongside her. Himself, the younger brother who, much of Ballyford and the surrounding countryside would agree, wasn't fit to shine his older brother Brian's shoes.

Yet . . . he had lived. While Brian, someone trusted and loved and respected by all, had died.

There were things in the world, Paddy knew, that made no sense at all. Plenty of them. But this one thing . . . this terrible truth . . . that Brian had died and Paddy had somehow lived, was the most nonsensical of them all.

"I just *loved* your article, Mr. Kelleher," an attractive middle-aged woman in a bright red cape gushed, holding out her hand. Paddy wasn't sure if he was expected to shake it or kiss it. He had no intention of kissing anyone's hand, so he shook it. She looked disappointed, but recovered quickly. "I understand you're doing a book for Edmund. He's my publisher, too, you know. I write poetry. For women."

"Men are not allowed to read it, then?" Paddy asked with a smile. "What, I wonder, might happen to them if they should sneak a peek at the pages?" A silly woman, this one, writer or not. As if poetry could be confined to only one segment of the population. Must not be very good verse, then.

The woman, who introduced herself as Margaret Lindsay Anderson, laughed. "I'm not sure, but I don't think we have to wonder about it. The covers of my little books are painted with flowers and pink ribbons. It's not likely that a man would have the courage to so much as pick up a copy, let alone glance inside it."

Though Paddy was unresponsive to her obvious flirting, Mrs. Anderson gushed on, intermittently annoying him further by asking questions he couldn't answer. When would the book he was writing for Edmund about that "tragic *Titanic* disaster" be in publication? Paddy had no idea. That depended upon how long it took him to write it, didn't it? And since he'd barely started it (though Edmund seemed to have the clear impression that Paddy was much further along in the manuscript), he couldn't even begin to guess how long that might be. He dreaded the moment when the publisher, who had such faith in him, might ask to see the completed pages. Belle, a college student, had been truly helpful with Paddy's grammar and spelling. Trouble was, she couldn't very well write the text for him. Trouble was, he couldn't, either. Leastways, it didn't seem to be happening. Every time he sat down with the big, lined tablet and the pile of sharpened pencils Belle had supplied him with, he was filled with dread. Stalling, he told Belle he didn't know where to start.

"Start at the beginning," Belle instructed gently. But then she left to attend her college classes, and Paddy had to wonder where the "beginning" might be? Would it be the morning when he and Brian and Katie left Ballyford forever, to make their way to Cobh Harbor to board the great, new, "unsinkable" ship? Or would the beginning be during that difficult but exciting journey from home by jaunting cart and lorry and on foot until the harbor came at last came into view? Maybe the "beginning" should be when they boarded the boat and were directed to the steerage accommodations, so much finer than they had expected. Their journey had truly begun then.

Or maybe all Edmund . . . all any reader was interested in, was the actual tragedy, from the moment on Sunday night when the iceberg, which must have been as big as a building, scraped the side of the *Titanic* and doomed everyone on it. Maybe, then, Sunday night should be the "beginning."

He wanted to ask Katie, so smart was she. But she would make him talk about it. If he was to concentrate on keeping the image of Brian out of his head, he maybe could *write* about it, as Edmund wanted him to. But he could *not* talk about it. If he did, something fierce-awful was bound to happen, Paddy knew it.

". . . And what sort of cover are you hoping for?" Mrs. Anderson babbled on.

Paddy looked at her as if he wondered who exactly she was talking to. And though the woman couldn't possibly have known it, he was wishing with all his heart that it was Katie Hanrahan's lovely face he was looking at instead of the poet Anderson's.

# Chapter 3

When Katie, as always, had sung her heart out, belting out "Oh, You Beautiful Doll" just the way she'd heard it sung on John Donnelly's phonograph, she was again quickly ushered to the door, this time by Pauly Chambers, a thin, balding agent in his sixties. He was kind enough about it, saying she had "a good set of pipes" and promising to give her a call. Nevertheless, the door was opened and Katie found herself on the other side of it as it swung shut.

But this time, before she had a chance to fight back tears of disappointment, she was stopped in her tracks by a loud voice bellowing, "Don't you be going nowheres, Missy! Stand right there where you are, just like that, while I take a good look at you."

The woman with the loud voice was overweight, her ample proportions stuffed into a shiny satin dress that made her look like an oversized orange. Her very curly hair was a brilliant shade of blond, and her long, pointed fingernails bore slashes of vivid scarlet that clashed violently with the dress. Lottie was staring openly and disapprovingly at the woman's makeup, and even Katie had to admit that while rouge and lip paint could often enhance features, on this woman they only exaggerated the wrinkles and puffiness of age.

But her eyes were a clear, bright blue, and she was smiling a warm, friendly smile at Katie. She had beautiful, white, even teeth. "Heard you belting out a tune in there for Pauly," she said. She shook her head. The curls bounced. "Pauly's right. You got a great set of pipes. But that song's all wrong for you."

Katie bristled. "'Tis a good song," she cried. "Everyone likes it. *I* like it!"

"Did I say it was a bad song? I said it was all wrong for you."

Lottie spoke up. "And who might you be? I thought the man inside was the theatrical agent."

A plump hand waved in dismissal. "He is. I'm Flo Chambers, the wife. I sit out here in the office and answer phones and write letters and handle hysterical clients. But take my word for it, I know as much about show business as he does. I used to be a performer, years ago. Did okay, too. And I'm telling you, this girl is going about things all wrong." She tapped an index finger against her teeth. "Where in heaven's name did you get that dress? You look like a wedding cake. It don't suit you at all. A plainer frock would be much better. And that hair!" She lifted a pudgy, jeweled finger. "You hiding something in there?" Laughing at her own wit, she ordered, "Take them pins out. Give 'em to me. Let that gorgeous red hair fall naturally, the way it was meant to. And then I want to hear you sing a few of them songs you sang back in the home country." She glanced down at a slip of paper on the desk behind her. "Hanrahan. Sing me an Irish tune, then." It sounded like a command, not a request.

"What's *wrong* with my dress?" Katie was close to tears. How could the woman be so cruel? "My aunt worked on it for weeks, gettin' it just right."

"Just right for a cheesy theater downtown," the woman said flatly. "That where you want to be, in some cheesy theater with men catcallin' at you? It's not where you belong, I can tell you that right off."

Katie stood up very straight, her head high. "I think where I belong should be up to me, don't you?"

Flo turned around and walked back to stand behind her desk. "Had a lot of calls, have you, then? People lining up around your place to pay you to sing for them?"

Cheeks very red, Katie stammered, "Well, no, but . . ."

"But nothin'. Like I said, you're taking the wrong approach. Kathleen, that your name?"

Katie nodded.

"Well, Kathleen, sing me a song you know as well as your own name."

Giving in, Katie did as she'd been told. She sang, "I'll Take You Home Again, Kathleen" in the same, sweet, true manner she had always sung it. And, as always, tears were shining in her eyes by the time she came to the end of the song. Though she loved it, it made her sad. Even more so now, because she knew exactly how that woman pining for her beloved Ireland felt.

When the last note ended, Katie failed to notice that the inner office door had swung open just a crack. What she did notice was the woman clapping her hands together in delight and saying, "There, that's it! Without that awful dress, with your hair down around your shoulders, and you singing that kind of song, I can keep you mighty busy. I can get you work all over the city, and that's a promise. Flo Chambers don't make promises she can't keep. I won't make you rich and I won't make you famous. You're not the type to be a headliner. But good, honest work, usin' the voice you was born with, that's nothin' to be stickin' your nose up at. I can book you in church halls and at picnics and private parties held by honest folk who won't be catcallin' at you, disrespectin' you. Might could even get you some stage work, though it won't be vaudeville. Vaudeville's not for you, dearie." She fixed her bright blue eyes on Katie. "So? Whadya say? You want the work or not?"

Stunned, Katie couldn't think. But the thought of telling Paddy that she was finally making some headway in her career was too tempting to resist. She said yes.

Only then did Pauly Chambers emerge from his office and admit grudgingly that his wife might "have something here." He wasn't all that happy about being upstaged, but he seemed perfectly willing to share in the commission Katie would be paying them out of her earnings. "Have her sing 'Harrigan' and 'Mother Macrae,'" he said brusquely. "People like 'em and they'd suit this girl." Then he retreated to his office again.

When Katie left, she was still dazed. But she was eager to call Paddy on the telephone and tell him her good news.

He wasn't home when she called.

John Donnelly, one of her aunt's boarders, a

nice, pleasant young man from County Down, *was* home, however. John had a good position in a bank, making enough money to send some home to his family with enough left over to buy himself some fine clothes and a phonograph, which he generously shared with Katie. John, too, suffered from occasional bouts of homesickness, and though he wasn't near as goodlooking or as interesting as Paddy, he was much easier to talk to. He understood how lonesome Katie got for her family and for Ireland. When it became especially painful, she went down the stairs to knock on John's door. They would talk for a while about their homeland, and then John would play for Katie the newest popular songs, so she could keep up with trends in the music business. He was very supportive of her ambition, and would have been willing to accompany her to auditions in New York had he not had a full-time job.

Paddy may not have been available, but John Donnelly was only too happy to listen to Katie's exciting news.

The Winslows' dining room table was perfection itself. The dinner service was white with a delicate blue fleur-de-lis pattern. The three centerpieces were lavish arrangements in shining golden urns, containing white orchids combined with deep blue flowers Elizabeth had never seen before. Probably flown in from some exotic land, she thought dryly. Betsy Winslow would never settle for flowers from the corner market. Flames from six gold candelabra, marching down the center of the mahogany table draped in pristine white linen, cast warm shadows over the scene.

As she ate, Elizabeth brooded about not being allowed to go to Max's apartment. But she met with him and his new friends in Central Park or in small cafes in the Village any time she could get away, which wasn't often. She loved the stimulating conversation, centering on politics, the state of the country, President Wilson, the condition of the poor in New York City, the dreadful state of the working class, including children as young as twelve who put in long hours in sweatshops. They talked about movies (which her mother still spoke of as the "cinematograph," saying it would "never last") and music and art. It was all interesting and stimulating and fun. Elizabeth took special pains to read *The New York Times* every day, so that she'd know something about what was going on in the world and wouldn't be left out of the conversations.

Had her mother ever been privy to any of those interesting discussions, she'd have tried to keep Elizabeth from ever taking part in them again.

The opportunity to see Max and his friends was arising less frequently these days. Her mother seemed to prefer Elizabeth's company more and more often over her own acquaintances, of whom there were many. And though there were many occasions when Elizabeth would have preferred anything to attending a function with her mother, she was reminded, always, of her promise to her father during those last, terrible moments on board the sinking ship. "Take care of your mother," he had said.

And so Elizabeth did.

But there were limits. "Mother," Elizabeth whispered later that evening, over the steady flow of polite dinner conversation, "how long do we have to stay? Can't we make an early exit, just this once? I have a headache."

That was a lie. She had no headache. But she was so bored. And she was cold. The Winslows' dining room was enormous, the blaze in the fireplace woefully inadequate for heating such a large room. As far as Elizabeth was concerned, they might as well have been eating outside on the terrace.

She couldn't stand the Winslows. Mrs. Winslow loved to brag that she possessed twenty-two place settings of the blue and white china, purchased on a recent trip to Italy. Elizabeth wondered if that meant Betsy Winslow and her husband were compelled to always invite twenty people to the frequent dinners they held in their Fifth Avenue mansion. She bit back a smile. If Mrs. Winslow occasionally invited only ten guests, perhaps she gave each of them two dinner plates, just to impress upon them that she owned twenty-two place settings.

Nola Farr shook her head in response to Elizabeth's request. "Don't be silly, dear. We're only on the second course. Dinner will last at least another hour and a half. Then we girls will go into the drawing room, the men into the library for brandy and cigars. We'll go home at ten-thirty, as always. Dessert is chocolate mousse, your favorite. And you know Betsy's cook is the best in the city."

When Elizabeth didn't answer, Nola continued, "You don't have plans to see Max tonight, do you, Elizabeth? Is that why you're so anxious to leave? It will be much too late when we get home. You have seen so little of him lately, I was wondering if that romance might not be dying." She sounded hopeful.

Well, there it is, Elizabeth told herself wearily. I'm not in the least surprised. I *knew* she was only pretending to accept Max. She hated the idea of the two of us together while we were on board the *Titanic*. Dead set against it. It wasn't until we got back here that she seemed to be all right with it. But she was simply lost in grief over Father and had no thought for anything else. Didn't I always suspect that she still disapproved?

Elizabeth thought in dismay, *That's* why she keeps me so busy, accompanying her everywhere, dragging me all over the city . . . to keep me away from Max. She's hoping I'll find someone more suitable, someone who isn't a struggling artist like Max. Someone *boring*, like Alan Reed. The only reason her mother never threw a fit over the broken engagement was, again, her grief.

Elizabeth was stricken by a horrible thought. Her mother wasn't hoping she would go back to Alan, was she? That would *never* happen. She had never loved Alan, never wanted the engagement. She wasn't even sure how it had happened. It had been her parents' idea. The three of them had battled about it all the way across the Atlantic. Until the ship hit the iceberg. . . .

Elizabeth had wished a thousand times since then that the crossing had been different for all of them. Wished that she could go back and *make* it different, with not one bitter word exhanged between herself and her father. If she had known those were going to be their *last* words. . . .

But she hadn't known. How could she? No one had. The *Titanic* had been thought unsinkable.

Those who thought it had been wrong.

Elizabeth seldom argued with her mother now, no matter how angry and frustrated she felt. Max thought she'd changed since the tragedy, lost her backbone. "Of course I've changed!" she had shouted at him tearfully, furious that he was criticizing her when what she really needed was understanding and kindness. "Who on board that ship hasn't changed since that night? Except you, of course," she had added harshly. "You go on with your life as if the *Titanic* never existed. But it did, Max! It did!"

They'd made up later, as they always had after an argument. Elizabeth had forgiven him by telling herself the difference between them was, Max hadn't lost someone dear to him when that ship went down. It was *she* who knew how quickly someone you loved could be taken away from you forever. She knew, now, that you needed to be careful, always, what you said to people you loved. You had to be careful how you treated them. It was true, her mother drove her insane, planning her social schedule right down to the very last minute, picking out her clothes, wanting Elizabeth always at her side. There were countless moments when she wanted to scream, "Leave me *alone*! Everything we do is so excruciatingly tiresome, I can't stand it! The parties, the dinners, the concerts, the dances, boring, boring, boring! Why can't you go places, do things, with your friends and let me live my *own* life?"

But she never said those things. She couldn't. Because perhaps then her mother would ask Joseph, their chauffeur, to drive her somewhere, and they might have an accident and her mother might be killed. Then those horrid words would be the last that Elizabeth and her mother ever exchanged.

She could not bear that thought.

"I'm sorry, Mother," she said quietly, "of course we'll stay for dessert. Chocolate mousse *is* my favorite. And the Winslows' cook *is* the best in the city."

She was completely unaware that her tone of voice was mechanical, totally devoid of any emotion. Or that she was parroting almost verbatim her mother's earlier words.

She was, however, aware that she was still very, very cold.

# Chapter 4

"But it's so *plain*!" Katie cried in dismay. "And it's so . . . so . . . *green*!"

Flo Chambers was holding up in front of her a bright green dress with long sleeves and a high neckline trimmed with a bit of ecru lace, but no other embellishments. This, she had explained to Katie and her aunt Lottie, was the gown she had decided Katie should wear for her singing engagements. "Green as a slice of Ireland, isn't it?" she had said proudly. She had picked it out herself, at the thrift shop down on the corner. "Hardly been worn at all, though," she had added quickly. "See for yourself, the hem's not even soiled. Clean as a whistle."

"Such a pretty color," Lottie offered, fingering the fabric. "Cotton, too. It'll be cool enough when the city heat hits, Katie."

Katie's lips turned down. Cotton! She wore cotton at home when she did her chores. She hadn't thought to be wearing it when she was out in public singing. What was wrong with the beautiful pink dress? It had taken her aunt three weeks to get that dress just right. And now Flo was replacing it with this plain, common frock? Singers were supposed to have some sophistication, everyone knew that. Flo was an agent's wife. She should know it better than anyone.

"Who's goin' to know I'm a singer, then?" she grumbled. In disgust, she flicked one sleeve of the dress, sending it flying up into Flo's face. "In *this* dress, I'm goin' to look like a peddler!"

Flo laughed, a deep, rumbling sound. "If it's a fancy costume you want, maybe vaudeville *is* the place for you. My guess is, you wouldn't last two minutes. You wouldn't like it, Kathleen. Take my word for it." She hung the dress on a wall hook and moved around behind her desk to ruffle through some papers. "Here," she said when she found what she was looking for, "I picked up some sheet music for you. These are the songs I think you should sing. And I've got you an engagement for Sunday night. An ice cream social put on by a Women's Club in Long Island. Rich people, so look your best."

Lottie protested. "I can't be takin' her all the way out there on Sunday night. I've got me ladies' church group that night."

Flo waved a plump hand. "Don't fret, Missus.

I drive, you know. None of my friends do, but then, their husbands see to it that they get where they're wanting to go. Pauly, he can't be bothered driving me all over the city, so he let me get my license, and he lets me take his car whenever I want. I'll be taking Katie where she needs to go, so you and your family needn't worry about her. She'll be safe enough with me."

Lottie sighed in relief, though her expression clearly said she disapproved of Flo driving "all over the city" alone.

Katie was relieved, too. But she didn't want to admit she'd been worried about how she was going to get herself from one place to another, so all she said was, "That'll be fine, then." Casting another contemptuous glance at the green dress, she added, "But I don't see why I can't wear my fine pink dress."

"Because you're not wanting to look like a strumpet, that's why," Flo said firmly, handing Katie three pieces of sheet music. "I've told the woman in charge of the social that you're a sweet, honest, Irish lass, and that's how you're going to present yourself. That's what they're paying you for."

Katie glanced up from the sheet music. "How much are they payin', then?"

Flo mentioned a figure. "Minus my commission, of course."

Katie subtracted mentally. There wasn't going to be a whole lot left for her. But then, hadn't Flo warned her right up front that she wasn't going to get rich? That was certain. She wasn't going to get that much attention at this affair, neither. People would be so busy eating ice cream at the social, they'd scarce listen to her at all. Back in Ireland, when she'd been imagining coming to America to be a singer, she had pictured herself on a stage in a famous concert hall in New York, every seat occupied by people who had come from all over to hear her sing. They would listen raptly, and it would be so quiet in the hall, you could hear the buzz of a bee. A noisy ice cream social had never been part of her fantasizing. There would be wee ones there, too, hundreds of them most likely, talking and playing so loud, she'd have to fairly shriek to make herself heard over their noise.

Katie's heart sank. The dress ... the engagement ... the money ... none of it was what she'd hoped for.

You're bein' sore ungrateful, she scolded mentally. Isn't Flo the very first person in America to give you a chance? Stop bein' so finicky and do what your da drummed into your head since you were knee-high ... do your best, no matter what it is you're doin'.

She would do her best, wee ones or no wee ones.

She turned her attention to the sheet music. And her heart sank again. "Oh, Flo," she wailed, waving the papers in the woman's face, "these are songs I been singin' my whole life! Can't I do somethin' different? Somethin' new? The songs John plays on his phonograph are so pretty. I sing them while I'm doin' chores, and all the boarders say how nice it sounds." Especially John. He loved her singing. He said it reminded him of home.

Flo sighed, but explained patiently, "I'm not selling you as a singer of popular songs, Katie. That's been your mistake all along, going to see agents and singing the same songs hundreds of other young girls sing. Anyone can sing that stuff. But not everyone can sing an Irish tune as if they'd wrote it themselves, as you can. Look again, there are a few popular songs in there. The two that Pauly mentioned, I got those for you. And I was thinking you should sing, 'When Irish Eyes Are Smiling.'" She grinned. "Could have been written just for you." Then she added dryly, "Though I have yet to see much in the way of smilin' eyes from you. But I can see that it's in you. You just haven't been in the mood yet. You will be, you'll see." More briskly, she went on, "And I especially want that piece you sang for me, that 'I'll Take You Home Again, Kathleen' in every performance. Maybe at the end. It can be your finale, what we call your signature song, the one everybody remembers long after the performance is over."

"But it makes me sad!"

"It'll make everybody sad. That's why they'll remember." Flo stood up. "Now, the social starts at seven on Sunday night. It'll take us a while to get there, so I'll be picking you up around five o'clock. That'll give you time to do some vocalizing before you sing. You can do it in the car on the way there if we're pressed for time. I won't mind."

It struck Katie then that this was actually going to happen. Butterflies assaulted her stomach. Never mind that it was just a little ice cream social, probably with more wee ones than grown-ups. Never mind that she wasn't going to be paid a fortune. She was going to be singing in public, in front of strangers, in America, for the very first time. What if she wasn't ready? What if they hated her? They might not be familiar with the songs Flo had picked. What if Flo was making a terrible mistake? If Katie sang the songs they all knew, wouldn't they like her better?

She didn't even know where Long Island *was*. Paddy and Belle and sometimes Edmund Tyree had taken her to Steeplechase Park on Coney Island, a wonderful fun place, and to the Statue of Liberty, and to the Astor Mansion on

Fifth Avenue, though of course they couldn't go inside, what with people living there. She had refused to go down into the subway, though Paddy had wanted her to. She never *would* go down there. But she'd been to the American Museum of Natural History, an amazing place with great wonders, and to Fifth Avenue to see the shops, though she hadn't bought a thing, with everything so dear. She liked just looking in the windows. Her second favorite place, after Coney Island, was Central Park, for the sheer greenery of it. She made Paddy take her there every chance she got. But she had not been to a place called Long Island.

Music in hand, Katie turned to leave.

Seeing the look on her face, Flo came out from behind her desk to pat Katie's shoulder and say, "Cheer up, dearie. There'll be better things comin' along than ice cream socials. Word will get around that Flo Chambers has a lovely little Irish girl ready to sing her heart out, and people will be askin' for you. Take my word for it. I'm never wrong about these things." She reached out and plucked the simple green dress off the wall. Smiling, she said lightly, "Don't forget this. You'll be wearin' it when I pick you up, won't you, Kathleen?"

Katie sighed heavily. "I will." The color *did* remind her of Ireland, just a bit. Not that she needed any reminding. Wasn't home and family always on her mind?

"Hair down on your shoulders, and no makeup to speak of, right?"

Another glum sigh. "Yes, ma'am."

Flo relented. "You can wear a bit of lipstick and a tiny bit of rouge, only because my guess is you'll have a touch of stage fright. That'll wash you out some. And you can powder your nose a bit so it's not too shiny. That wouldn't do."

Katie perked up a bit. With a bit of makeup on her face, the green dress might not seem so plain.

On the way home, she decided Paddy should come to see her first public performance. Heaven knew she'd gone to enough of them snooty literary gatherings with him. His new friends weren't all that nice to her, either. They always asked her what she "did" in New York, and when she answered that she hoped to be a singer, some laughed, some turned away in dismissal, some said, "Oh, doesn't everyone these days?" At one afternoon tea, a young woman with bobbed hair the color of lemons had asked, "And are you a writer like our darling Paddy?" Katie, bored and feeling out of place had snapped, "No, but if I was, I wouldn't be wastin' my time at parties like our *darlin'* Paddy is doin', I'd be home doin' some writin'!"

Paddy had overheard and been insulted. They'd had a terrible argument, and hadn't made peace for a whole miserable week.

He owed her for all those long afternoons and evenings spent in the company of them bookish snobs. *She* read books. She loved to read. They didn't need to treat her like she was simple-minded.

If Paddy didn't come to her ice cream social, they just might have another argument.

Actually, now that she thought about it, they seemed to be fighting a lot these days. Her aunt Lottie, who, like most women, had fallen under Paddy's spell immediately and adored him, said placatingly, "You're just adjustin' to the new country, that's all, Katie. And you've both been through a turrible time. Be patient, it'll work itself out."

But patience wasn't Katie's strong suit.

She wanted Paddy to do well. To be a great writer. She knew he could tell wonderful stories. Hadn't he kept her and Brian entertained all the way from Ballyford to Cobh Harbor with his fine story-telling? But she didn't see how going to all them parties and dinners and meetings was helping him get the words written down on paper. She had asked him, not long ago, how the book about the *Titanic* was coming along. He had fairly bitten her head off. "I can't talk about that," he had said, his voice harsh. "I need to save all my thoughts about that night for the book. Was I to keep talkin' and talkin' and talkin', like *you've* a mind to, there'd be nothin' left inside for puttin' down on paper."

Her feelings hurt, she had said indignantly, "I didn't *ask* you to talk about that night, I *asked* you how the book was coming. And it seems to me, if you really *was* puttin' words down on paper, you wouldn't be gettin' so mad when I ask you about it."

He'd been so angry, he'd stalked off. She hadn't seen him again that afternoon. Belle had had to send her home in Edmund's car. When he finally called on the telephone, Katie hadn't apologized. She had barely spoken two words to him until *he* said he was sorry. Which he did, though he took his own sweet time about it. And mumbled something about how "hard" writing was.

Katie had been unsympathetic. How would Paddy know writin' was hard when he wasn't doing that much of it?

Still, he was making progress in his career, and she was getting nowhere.

But that was before she met Flo.

Maybe Paddy would call on the telephone tonight. She couldn't wait to tell him about the ice cream social. He didn't call that often, though Edmund had seen to it that he had a telephone, saying he wanted to be able to get in touch with Paddy when he needed to. The only telephone Katie had access to was in the front hall of the roominghouse. She had precious little privacy when she was talking on it. But she was always so glad to hear Paddy's voice, she didn't care.

If Paddy didn't call, she might just go talk to John. He'd show some interest. He might even offer to accompany her on Sunday, to give her moral support, hear her sing, and eat ice cream all at the same time. John liked simple pleasures. It would serve Paddy right if she invited John to the social. And maybe if he knew there was another gentleman, an Irish one at that, paying some mind to Kathleen Hanrahan, he'd call her more often and come out to Brooklyn to see her more than once a week.

Or . . . Katie shifted restlessly in her seat . . . maybe he wouldn't. Maybe he'd just say, "Well fine then, Miss Kathleen Hanrahan, you just go right ahead and cozy up to your John Donnelly. I've me own friends now, and Belle Tyree is a fine-lookin' woman with a pleasin' attitude and no bad temper to speak of, and that's the truth of it."

Tears sprang to Katie's eyes. If Paddy ever said that, her heart would crack right down the middle like the great ship *Titanic*. If he ever said that, she wouldn't be so glad that she had survived the terrible disaster. Not so glad at all.

"Why, Katie-girl," her aunt Lottie said, leaning forward to touch Katie's arms, "you've tears in your eyes. Are you not happy about singin' in public, then?"

"'Course I am. I'm just . . . a bit nervy, that's all. Stage fright, like Flo said. It'll pass. I've sung in public before, Aunt Lottie, back home." Where everyone knew me, and everyone was kind, Katie thought but didn't say. "I'll be right as rain by Sunday, that's certain."

But in her heart, Katie knew she would only be right as rain if Paddy was there to cheer her on.

Elizabeth didn't see Max for a few days. When he telephoned, he said he was busy painting. But Saturday afternoon, shortly after lunch, he rang the doorbell at the mansion on Murray Hill. When Elizabeth, still in tennis whites from a match with her mother on their backyard court, answered the doorbell instead of Esther, the housemaid, Max's eyebrows went up. "Don't tell me, let me guess. You've let all the servants go. From now on, you and your mother are going to do the housekeeping."

Elizabeth laughed. "Can you see my mother wielding a dusting cloth?"

"No more than I can see *you* buying lettuce at a produce stand."

Elizabeth bristled, but she let him in. "I know how to buy lettuce. You . . . you thump it to make sure it's fresh."

It was Max's turn to laugh. "That's melon, Elizabeth, not lettuce."

With a careless shrug, Elizabeth led him into the sun room and flung herself down on a white wicker settee plump with green flowered cushions. April sunshine spilled in through the window and across the gleaming hardwood floor, warming her. This was her favorite room, because it was seldom as cold as the larger rooms. And because her father's desk was still in here, just as he'd left it. She felt closer to him in this room.

She smiled at Max. "If you think I'm so spoiled and stupid, what are you doing here?"

He sat down beside her and put a comforting arm around her shoulders. "I do not think you're stupid. Far from it. And I'm here because I think," he said calmly, "that you're bright and clever and interesting, and you have a warm heart. I like a warm heart. Especially when that warm heart likes me back." Smiling, he peered into her face with eyes so deep a blue they reminded Elizabeth of the ocean. That unsettled her, and she pulled away. She didn't want to be reminded of the ocean.

But Max persisted. "You *do* still like me back, don't you, Elizabeth? Say it! Or I'll go back home and paint all day instead of beating you at tennis."

She aimed a questioning glance at his gray slacks and blue sweater. "You can't play tennis in those clothes."

"I brought whites. They're in my car."

His *car*? Elizabeth squealed and bolted upright. "Your car? You bought a car? Oh, Max, what fun! Let me see it!" She jumped up and ran to the door, yanking it open. Without waiting to see if he was behind her, she ran down the steps. The car was parked at the curb. It was quite new, its paint shiny black, its upholstery white. There was a small glass vase attached near the window, and Max had already filled it with a single pink rose.

Clapping her hands in delight, Elizabeth cried, "And it's all *yours*?" She whirled to throw her arms around his neck, without a thought for disapproving passersby. "I thought you said no one needed a car in the city."

"Changed my mind. If I ever decide to do landscapes again, I'll need a car to go exploring the countryside. And," he said, grinning, "this'll make it easier to see you, too. It's a Kettering. No cranking. Don't have to worry about fracturing my painting arm. Want to go for a spin?"

"You bet! Wait'll I run in and tell Moth —"

Elizabeth stopped speaking abruptly, and frowned. "Oh, no. I just remembered. We're to meet with the dressmaker in forty-five minutes. Mother's bathing, and I'm supposed to be doing the same." Disappointment clouded her face.

Max leaned against the car, his arms folded over his chest. He was no longer smiling. "The dressmaker? You'd rather be stuck with pins than go for a ride in my new car?"

"No, of course I wouldn't." Elizabeth looked longingly at the car. "But we have this appointment, and Madame Claude-Pierre is not someone you break appointments with. She's French, you know. Not exactly the soul of patience."

"Why can't your mother go alone?" He didn't add, "For a change," but Elizabeth heard it in his voice.

"They're my clothes, too, Max. It's spring. I can't wear my winter clothes in the springtime." This struck Elizabeth as very ironic, because she would have preferred to continue wearing the warmer winter clothes. But if she admitted that to Max, he'd tell her again that she should see a doctor about her constant chill, as he had at Christmas. "And my mother would be very upset if I said I wasn't going. You know how she gets."

He shrugged. "Okay. If you don't want to

take a ride in my new car, I guess I'll go home and paint."

"I'm sorry, Max." She was *very* sorry. But her mother's reaction if Elizabeth said she wasn't going to the dressmaking appointment would be much worse than Max's reaction. Max never overreacted the way Nola did. Or maybe he was just becoming accustomed to her choosing her mother over him. He did *not* look happy, though. "You could come back later," she suggested. "We should be home by three. Or we could go tomorrow afternoon."

"That's half the afternoon gone, three o'clock," Max said, his voice cool. "And I think it's going to rain tomorrow." He shrugged again. "Your mother probably has something planned, anyway." Without a good-bye kiss, he moved away from Elizabeth, around the front of the car to climb into the driver's seat. When he was behind the wheel, he added, "I hope you've noticed that I'm not arguing about this. But it's not because I don't care. It's because I know it would be a waste of time. But you know what, Elizabeth? I don't for a minute believe your father meant you should give up your whole life. I don't think he'd want you to do that."

"Max . . ." Elizabeth was close to tears. It was a wonderful car, and the thought of spending the whole, sunny afternoon riding around in it at Max's side was exactly what she wanted to do. It would make her feel happy again, and young and carefree, things she hadn't felt in a very long time. Not since . . . no, she wasn't going to think about that. Anger was a much safer emotion, so she let it flare up. "You should have telephoned first!" she called heatedly as he pulled away slowly. "That's the proper thing to do."

But the sound of the car's engine drowned out her words.

And then Max was pulling away, chugging off down the street without her.

Elizabeth whirled and ran inside, tears of frustration stinging her eyes.

# Chapter 5

To Katie's bitter disappointment, Paddy failed to make it to the ice cream social on Long Island. He had promised to be there. "Wouldn't miss it," he said when she finally reached him on the telephone on Thursday afternoon.

But he did miss it.

And although he telephoned her later to apologize, sounding genuinely regretful and using the excuse that Edmund had called him Sunday afternoon to say there was a new agent he wanted Paddy to meet with that evening, Katie refused to forgive him. "If you'd really wanted to be there to hear me sing," she told him scornfully, "you'da been there. That's all I know." And she'd hung up, slamming the receiver into its wall hook with so much force she nearly broke the cord.

It wasn't as if she hadn't enjoyed the social. But it would have been much better if Paddy had been sitting at one of the large, white, round tables arranged on the lush green lawns, listening attentively as she sang.

Long Island was so much prettier than Brooklyn, shaded by huge old trees and carpeted in velvety green grass. Even the spring air seemed fresher, and though the drive was tiring, it was exciting to be in a nice, big car with the breeze blowing around them. Flo seemed a good driver, as if she'd been doing it all her life instead of only a year or two, as she admitted to Katie. The social was held at a fine estate in a place called Garden City, where every home seemed to be grander than the next. The grounds were near as big as all of Ballyford, with plenty of room for over a hundred tables with matching white chairs. To Katie's amazement, the hostess had hired an orchestra to accompany her, and to play for the guests when Katie wasn't singing.

At home, an ice cream social was held most often at the church, to raise money. Everyone in town came, bought ice cream, ate it, did some socializing, maybe some singing, then went home. So Katie had expected people to be coming and going all evening, which she knew she would find unsettling. It would be hard to concentrate on the words of the new songs with people jumping up and skedaddling every few minutes.

But it wasn't like that. To her surprise, all of the guests had been invited, as if it were a party. They arrived on time and stayed all evening, sitting quietly in their seats, ice cream dishes in front of them and perhaps a coffee cup or two, while Katie sang. Flo explained that these were all wealthy people who had already donated generously to the Women's Club.

They were just as generous with their applause.

Once Katie got over her disappointment about Paddy not showing up, she spent the rest of the evening between songs studying the dress and manners of the ladies. Such finery! She'd never seen anything like the sheer, pastel-colored dresses, the jewelry, the shoes. Not even on the *Titanic*, where she'd been confined to third class. There'd been that one morning, though, when she and a friend had been permitted to attend a church service in the first-class dining room. But that had been a solemn occasion, not festive like this event, and she had noticed only that the pretty girl was there, wearing a fine woolen navy blue suit.

Here on Long Island, she liked the way the women sat at their tables, with their hands folded in their laps, or perhaps a hand under the chin to show attentiveness, their legs daintily crossed at the ankle, showing the pretty shoes dyed to match their dresses. She tried to imitate their posture and movements when she relaxed between songs, leaving the round white stage that had been constructed in the middle of the lawn to take a seat at one of the tables with Flo.

"You're doin' super, honey," Flo said, patting Katie's hand. "They're crazy about you. Didn't I tell you? And there are some big shots here, too, who might be throwing parties or dances, might be asking you to sing at some of them. I bet they'd be willing to pay a pretty penny, too, although," she said, lowering her voice, "sometimes it's the richest ones that's the tightest with their dough, know what I mean?"

Katie didn't. A waiter in a white jacket brought her, unbidden, a white china dish heaped high with creamy white ice cream. She started to thank him, but Flo's warning glance stopped her. He's just doing his job, her blue eyes signalled, no need to thank him.

The ice cream was vanilla, Katie's favorite. "I guess," she said slowly as she ate, "you'd have to be very rich to live out here, wouldn't you?" She was thinking, if Paddy ever wrote his book about the *Titanic* and it sold a lot of copies and made lots of money, maybe. . . .

"You bet." Flo, her bulk encased in a bright yellow gown, glanced around at the other tables. "Some here might be bankers. But mostly, I think they're just folks who've always had money. Never even did anything to earn it, I'd guess. Just got it from the day they was born, because their folks had it. The cream of New York, that's who you're singing for tonight, Katie."

"Might there be any writers living on Long Island, do you think?"

Flo laughed. "Writers? Not likely. Have to sell one heck of a lot of books to buy a house out here. I told you, Katie, these people don't *work*. They don't have to."

Disappointed, Katie sat lost in thought until time for her next song. Garden City was closer to how she had imagined America. No one had told her that Brooklyn would have so little green to it, so few trees, so many buildings so close together, so many people living in those buildings.

When Katie sang, "I'll Take You Home Again, Kathleen" at the end of the evening, the tears in her eyes were very real. And although many eyes in the crowd listening to her were wet as well, those tears came from sentiment, not yearning, as hers did.

She was about to leave when a distinguished-looking gentleman in a tuxedo came up to her to shake her hand, compliment her on her voice, and ask if she would be available to sing at his wife's birthday party in Manhattan, two weeks hence on Saturday night. The address he gave was Riverside Drive, which meant nothing to Katie. She referred him to Flo, standing nearby, and the arrangements were made.

They were barely settled in the car when Flo chuckled to herself and announced, "I told him your fee was a hundred dollars!"

Katie gasped. "You didn't!"

"I sure did. He never blinked an eye. Just nodded as if he was saying, Of course it is, and said we should be there by eight that Saturday night. Riverside Drive, a fine neighborhood. You're doing all right for yourself, Kathleen, my girl. Didn't I say so?" As she drove away from the estate, Flo confided, "With his type, you've gotta jack up the price a little, make them think they're getting more. They're used to walking into Tiffany's and laying down a couple thousand every month or so, you know? They *like* spending money. Makes them feel powerful, I'd guess."

Katie couldn't imagine spending "a couple thousand" dollars even once a year, let alone once a month. Not likely that she'd ever have that kind of money. And if she did, she wouldn't spend it at Tiffany's. She'd save it until she had enough to buy a house on Long Island, not even such a big, fancy one like the one tonight. Maybe there were smaller, plainer houses out there somewhere.

Flo chuckled again. "Well, kiddo, looks to me like you're on your way. Maybe we ought to spring for another frock. Can't keep wearing that same one if you're going to be as busy as I think you are. And with a hundred-dollar fee, I guess we can come up with a bit of a wardrobe for you. Nothing fancy, though," she warned before Katie could say anything. "Remember, you're a simple Irish girl. That's what they're buying, so that's what we're selling. No ruffles or geegaws, just plain frocks, that's the ticket."

Katie still hadn't responded.

Flo glanced over at her. "You okay? I'd think you'd be floating six feet off the ground, the way those people carried on over you. How come you've gone all quiet on me? You just weary?"

Katie was grateful for the ready excuse Flo had given her. She nodded. "Seems like. I was too nervy to sleep much last night." Anything was better than telling Flo how sad she was that she would never live on beautiful Long Island, and how disappointed she was that Paddy hadn't come to share in her triumph. Flo would think the first thought was crazy because only rich people lived on Long Island. She would think the second thought was stupid because she didn't hold with ladies letting men sour their lives. "Pauly never gets in *my* way," she had told Katie on the drive out. "I do as I please. If he doesn't like it, he can go fly a kite in Central Park."

Laying her head back on the seat, Katie closed her eyes, thinking, I should have invited John to come along tonight. Why didn't I, then? I meant to.

Because, she answered herself silently, it wasn't John I wanted there. It was Paddy.

# Chapter 6

The Brooklyn neighborhood where Katie's aunt and uncle lived was not a wealthy one. It was very different from the pictures of America she'd seen in books. The tall, narrow, frame buildings, many of them roominghouses, seemed worn and tired to her, as if they were too tired to stand up straight. Postage-stamp backyards were nearly taken up completely by wet garments flapping like flags on clotheslines strung between two metal poles. The children played, for the most part, in the street. Their voices rang out throughout the hot, sticky summer days, then slacked off when school began in the fall. On summer evenings, with windows open to let in whatever scant breeze might be about, adult voices raised in harsh argument often drowned out the sounds of children playing stickball or hide-and-go-seek or kick-the-can. The smells of laundry soap and cooking hung heavy in the air, sometimes giving Katie a headache. Heavy feet hammered up and down wooden staircases, the iceman's shrill, demanding voice rang out, bells on wagons passing in the street below echoed throughout the day. Brooklyn, New York, America, was not a quiet, restful place. Not to Katie. And there was no cooling breeze from nearby trees, because there were virtually *no* trees on their avenue, nor was there a clear, sparkling stream in which to go wading.

To ease her homesickness, Katie made friends in the neighborhood. One of her favorites was Mary Donohue, only three years older than Katie and fresh from Ireland with her young husband Tom and their four-year-old daughter, Bridget. They lived in Agnes Murphy's roominghouse, across the street. Mary was prone to spells of depression, during which she would lie on the davenport in the tiny, darkened living room, a wet cloth on her forehead, leaving Bridget's care to neighbors. But when she wasn't in the throes of melancholia, she was great fun, full of life and laughter, and teasing Katie about Paddy. "Aye, a handsome lad he is," she exclaimed when she first saw him, "but are you sure he's not goin' to break your heart, then?"

Since that was the one thing Katie was *not*

sure of, she snapped, "Sure and a fellow can only break your heart if you let him, which I ain't about to do!"

Mary just laughed.

Katie and Bridget were sitting on Mary's front porch on the Wednesday after the ice cream social, Katie brushing Bridget's hair while Mary slept inside on the davenport, when a taxicab pulled up in front of her aunt's house and Paddy unfolded himself from the back seat. Katie knew it was him even before he got out. No one in the neighborhood could afford taxicabs, but Paddy often arrived in one. Just as often, Edmund sent him to Brooklyn in a chauffeur-driven car. "You're the only one who can settle him down," the publisher had told Katie at a recent party, "so whatever it takes to get him out there to see you, that's what I'll do."

Not that she'd had much luck "settling" Paddy down lately.

As always when she saw him, her breath caught in her throat. Even when, as now, she was furious with him, her first instinct whenever he appeared was to rush to him and throw herself into his arms. Thank the stars she'd been raised not to behave so unladylike, or it would be a fool she'd be making of herself, right there in the streets of Brooklyn.

He saw her sitting on Mary's steps and loped across the street in that lazy, arrogant way he had.

He didn't come to my social, Katie reminded herself firmly, refusing to stand up and greet him. He had more important things to do.

But half an hour later, wearing a fresh white middy and firmly holding Bridget's hand, Katie was climbing into another cab and heading for Manhattan with Paddy. "I'm takin' the afternoon off from writin'," he'd said excitedly, "and you're comin' with me into the city. The wee one can come along, if you've a mind to bring her. She should see the big city, anyways."

When Katie asked what they would be doing when they got to the city, Paddy shook his handsome head. "'Tis a surprise."

Paddy hadn't said a word about her ice cream social. He hadn't apologized for not showing up, and he hadn't even asked her how it had been. It was as if it hadn't happened. And Katie was too stubborn to bring it up herself. Anyways, that would just start an argument, and she didn't want to ruin the day for Bridget, who was staring out the taxicab window with huge brown eyes. Her parents had not yet taken her to the city, and she was trying to take in everything at once. She was impressed by the Brooklyn Bridge, which Katie thought ugly but preferred to the riverboats, feeling the way she did about boats now. Paddy pointed out the top of the Woolworth Building, the tallest in the world.

"How do people get to the top of it?" Bridget, nearly hanging out the taxicab's window, asked breathlessly.

"The tallest buildings have elevators," Katie answered, her heart pounding at the thought of the dreaded iron cages. "And all of them have stairs, just like you do at your house."

Though Katie disliked the hustle and bustle of New York City, Bridget seemed to love it. "So many people," she declared, "and so many cars and big buildings. How come the ground don't cave in?"

Katie's worry exactly.

Paddy directed the driver to their final destination. When it pulled up in front of Grand Central Station and stopped, Katie was delighted. Grand Central was a fair interesting place. Twice on a Saturday afternoon, she and Paddy had whiled away several happy hours doing nothing more than sitting on benches watching people hurry by. Paddy called it "gatherin' writin' material." Imagining what kind of lives different people led, where they lived, what their occupation might be, where they were going to or coming from, was, he said, "food for writin'."

Katie just thought it great fun.

"Oh, you're goin' to like this," she told Bridget as they climbed from the cab and the driver sped away. "You'll see more people inside here than you'll see in a month of Sundays in Brooklyn. 'Tis a great place to see how New Yorkers dress and hear how they talk as they hurry past."

But when they were inside, instead of leading them to a centrally located bench where they'd be sure to have a good view of passersby hurrying to and from the trains, Paddy kept walking.

"Where are you goin'?" Katie asked, her eyes on a particularly well-situated bench. If they didn't position themselves on it quickly, someone else might take it.

He turned to face her. "I've a surprise for you. We're goin' to take a train ride. You haven't yet, and today seemed like a good day. Bridget will love it." Paddy took the little girl's hand in his. "So will you, Katie. It'll be an adventure." Smiling, he looked deep into her eyes. "We haven't been seein' enough of each other, didn't you say so yourself? A nice, quiet train ride is just the ticket." He laughed. "Ticket? Maybe I'm gettin' better at playin' around with words."

Katie frowned, uncomprehending.

"You need a ticket to get on the train," Paddy explained. "Come on now, we're wastin' time."

But when Paddy had purchased three tickets to a destination he refused to reveal, he motioned Katie toward a set of wide steps leading downward.

She stopped walking. *Down?* He was taking them *down? Belowground?* Her stomach twisted, and her palms grew clammy. No ... *no ...* she couldn't!

Realizing she wasn't following, Paddy stopped and turned around, as did Bridget. "Come on, then, our train leaves in six minutes."

Katie didn't move. "We have to go down?"

He frowned. "The trains are down there. They come in through tunnels forty feet underground. Amazin', ain't it? Come on, then."

Katie gasped. Forty feet underground? Tunnels? She broke out in a cold sweat. She took a step backward, nearly bumping into a couple hurrying toward the stairs. "You didn't say it was underground."

Paddy sighed impatiently. "It ain't underground the whole way. Not like the subway. I know you'd hate that. The trains only come in and out underground, that's all. Just a few minutes, and then you're up top, honest."

Katie tried. Paddy had taken this time for her, and she wanted to have a good time. And Bridget seemed excited about the prospect of a train ride.

So she went down one step...two... three ... people hurried past her, far more anxious than she to descend ... four ... now the darkness below was visible, staring up at her as if to say, Go ahead, then, come on down so I can swallow you up. Hurry, so I can close in on you like the walls of a coffin.

Katie stopped on the fifth step down. Her legs felt like jelly, and her hands were shaking. "I'm not going down there, Paddy. I can't." What was the *matter* with him? Had he forgotten the torturous time she'd spent in the subterranean passageways of *Titanic*, trying to find a way up top? He knew all about it. Wasn't he the one, then, who had found her? He'd *seen* the state she was in. He knew better than anyone how impossible it was for her to be closed in now. And since he wasn't an ignorant lout, he had to know how much worse it would be for her to be enclosed in something that was *belowground*. The thought of a tunnel, dark and narrow, made her physically ill. "I can't go down there. Take me home, Paddy. Take Bridget and me home."

He was at her side then, looking genuinely puzzled. "Katie, it's just a train ride. People take them all the time." He waved his hands to encompass the stream of would-be passengers hurrying past them on the stairs. "The trains are perfectly safe."

She backed up another step. She was trembling. "No, they're not. That's not true. I'm reading in the *Herald* almost every day about train accidents." That was true enough. "And people say they're bumpy and noisy and..." But none of that had anything to do with it. If the train hadn't been underground, if it hadn't entered through a tunnel, she would have tried it, just for the adventure of it. She hated being afraid of things, and never had been before. Never. But she wasn't going down into that black tunnel. Not now. Not ever.

"We're not going to have an accident." Paddy's tone was patient enough, but he was tapping the three tickets against one hand impatiently. "Do you think I'd be takin' you and little Bridget here on a train if I wasn't thinkin' it was safe, then? Wouldn't that make me some kind of callous brute? I was just thinkin', this is the best way for you to get over your fear of bein' belowground. Can't be like that forever, you know."

So he *hadn't* forgotten her terror. Somehow that made it worse. Why should Paddy Kelleher be deciding how she was supposed to get over something? What did he know about such things?

He softened his voice in that way he had when he wanted something and he thought the other person was being unreasonable in not granting it. "Katie-girl, we're in the big city now. This ain't Ballyford, where the only way to get around is by jaunting cart or lorry. Isn't it grand, then, that they got trains right here in the city?"

Katie lost her temper. "'Tis cruel of you to be remindin' me this ain't Ballyford, when you know full well that's where I'd rather be! And I'm *not* goin' down into any black underground tunnel, Patrick Kelleher. You take us home right now, or I'll get us there meself!" Though she had no idea how. She'd brought no money with her. Hadn't thought she'd need any, since Edmund always saw to it that Paddy had plenty in his pockets. If she had to, she'd find a telephone somewheres and call Flo. Flo would get her and Bridget home, even if she had to drive them there herself.

Paddy knew Katie well enough to sense when it would be easier to move the Brooklyn Bridge than to change her mind. He gave up, and they turned and went back up the steps and outside.

No one suggested that they sit on a bench and people watch.

The fresh air felt wonderful to Katie.

But the cab ride home was a silent one. A confused Bridget stared solemnly out the window, Paddy sat as far away from Katie as possible, and Katie herself fought angry tears. She wanted to tell Paddy how she felt, how hurt she was that he had tried to push her into "gettin' over" her terror. Wasn't that easy, was it? She couldn't help the way her stomach started to hurt and her chest ached and she couldn't breathe and she broke out in a cold sweat when she found herself in a small, enclosed space, especially one underground. Didn't do it on purpose, did she, then? If she could stop it, she would.

She wanted to tell Paddy how she felt, how hurt she was that he hadn't come to the social. She wanted him to know how upset she was that he'd expected her to descend those stone steps into the darkness of a narrow tunnel. But she didn't want to talk about those things in front of Bridget or the taxicab driver.

Paddy would probably drop them off in Brooklyn and speed away without so much as a good-bye, and she'd never get the chance to say what she felt. He was probably thinking that here he'd taken time away from his busy life in the city to spend an afternoon with her, and she'd gone and ruined it. Probably blaming her. He wouldn't take an afternoon off again any time soon, not for her.

When they pulled up in front of the rooming-house, Paddy got out to silently hold the door open for Katie and Bridget. Spotting Mary sitting on their steps, looking healthy and refreshed, Bridget cried out and ran to her.

"I'm sorry I ruined the fine afternoon you'd planned," Katie said quietly, looking up into Paddy's face with pained eyes. "But I'm not ready to be ridin' along underground in a dark tunnel. I'd think you'd know that."

His eyes avoiding hers, he shrugged. "Could be I was wrong," he said reluctantly, surprising her. Being wrong was not something Paddy Kelleher admitted readily. "Askin' too much of you, could be." He looked down at her then, concern on his handsome face. "You was shakin' somethin' fierce, Katie. Just like down there in the *Titanic* when I came across you and the wee ones. I didn't know it was still that bad." Then, even though it was broad daylight, even though Mrs. Toomey and Mrs. Costello were sitting on their front porches, and Mary and Bridget and Mrs. Murphy on theirs, and even though there were children playing stickball in the street, Paddy took Katie into his arms and kissed her for all the world to see. "I'm the one who's sorry," he murmured into her ear. "I wasn't thinkin' clear, and that's the truth. And I'm sorry I missed your singin' Sunday night, too. Doesn't seem like I'm much good to you these days. Don't know why you put up with me. Was I as bright as me brother was, you'd be a sight better off."

Surprised, Katie pulled away from him. He

had never talked like that before. Hadn't even mentioned Brian in months. It was one thing for *her* to think that Paddy Kelleher wasn't much use to her these days, what with him so busy in the city and all. But it sounded odd to hear him giving voice to the very same thought. It wasn't like him, not like him at all. Confused, she said softly, "I love you just the way you are, Paddy. Why would I be wishin' you was somebody else?"

Mary and Bridget had clapped loudly when Paddy kissed Katie. Aware of eyes still upon them, Katie added, "Come on inside then. We can talk about Bri if you want, or about us if that's what you're wantin'. I do want to tell you all about Flo and the places she's goin' to have me sing. We *need* to talk, Paddy."

At first she thought he might say yes. He seemed to hesitate, even take a step forward. But when she said "Bri," his eyes clouded, and he shook his head. "Can't just now," he said. "Got to get back. There's some 'do' tonight I'm supposed to go to. But I'll telephone you later, if I get home in time." He kissed her on the cheek, then stepped around her to enter the cab.

Mary and Bridget were smiling as the cab pulled away. Katie wasn't. Because Paddy had taken the afternoon off for a train trip, but they hadn't *taken* that train trip. So why was it he couldn't have used all that time left over for a talk with her, when she was needing it so sorely?

Because he didn't want to, came the disheartening answer.

And on the heels of that came an even more disturbing thought. He still thought she'd have been better off with Brian? After all this time, after everything they'd been through together? How could he be thinking that?

What was *wrong* with Paddy?

# Chapter 7

"I have never been so mortified in my life! My own daughter, falling asleep in the middle of a performance, for all the world to see. Elizabeth, how *could* you! Mrs. Schermin was staring at you. I'm sure she must think I've raised you with no appreciation for the arts whatever."

"I don't care what she thinks. The opera was boring. If we'd gone to see the Castles the way I wanted, I wouldn't have fallen asleep. It would have been more fun. I wasn't tired, I was bored."

Nola sniffed in disdain. "Vernon and Irene Castle are vulgar. Their dancing is vulgar, I don't care how popular they are. Perhaps I *did* raise you with no appreciation for the arts."

Elizabeth leaned back against the car seat. "I don't want to argue, Mother. I'm sorry I embarrassed you. Maybe next time you should go with your friends and I'll stay home with a good book." Or go visit Max and his friends in Greenwich Village. She hadn't seen any of them in a while. She missed the lively discussions. And she missed Max fiercely. She so seldom saw him these days. He was busy, and her mother certainly kept *her* busy.

A breeze caressed Elizabeth's cheeks as Joseph drove homeward. She envied the young couples she saw strolling along Madison Avenue holding hands. Others rode by in horse-drawn hansom cabs. Elizabeth sighed. When had she last enjoyed a nice, romantic evening?

It shocked her to realize that the last truly romantic evening she'd shared with Max had been . . . on the *Titanic*. Although they had been together many times during the year since they'd returned to New York, they were seldom alone. Nola was always there, always present. Even when they *were* alone, however briefly, it just wasn't the same. The terrible events of that night lay between them, a chasm neither one of them seemed able to leap across. Would it ever go away? Or, like the icebergs no doubt still floating treacherously in the North Atlantic, would it always be there?

It's my fault, Elizabeth thought clearly. I'm the one who's changed the most since we got back. On the ship, I had such plans, such dreams, and I was so determined to fulfill them. Max liked that, he applauded it. He *wanted* me to strike out on my own, though I had no idea how I would do that. He had done it, and he seemed so certain that I could, too, though he never understood just how difficult it would be. Still, he had faith in me, maybe more than I had in myself. Now, where are my plans? What have I done with them? Why don't I have them anymore?

Perhaps they had sunk with the *Titanic*.

That thought disturbed Elizabeth. Because nothing that sank with the ship had been resurrected.

"We must begin making plans for Atlantic City," Nola said, pulling Elizabeth away from her thoughts. She spoke as if she had completely dismissed the humiliation of a daughter who fell asleep at the opera. "You know how busy the Marlborough is in July. And we wouldn't want to stay anywhere else."

"I'm not going." The words fell out of Elizabeth's mouth. She hadn't meant to say them, wasn't even aware of having thought them, yet there they were.

"*What* did you say?"

Elizabeth took a deep breath, let it out. "I said, I'm not going to Atlantic City. Or to the Jersey Shore or to Long Island. I'm not. I have ... I have other things to do this summer."

Nola laughed, a harsh sound in the darkened

interior of the car. "Such as, pray tell? You have no plans that *I'm* aware of." The implication being that if Elizabeth *did* have plans, her mother would certainly know of them.

"Well, that's the problem, Mother, right there. The idea that I shouldn't have any plans that you don't know about. Like I have no life of my own. You just admitted as much." They were within two minutes of the Murray Hill house. It wasn't likely that the discussion would continue when they got home. Nola would go to her room, and tomorrow morning she'd be talking about Atlantic City again as if Elizabeth had never opened her mouth. "Don't you think that's rather sad, that an eighteen-year-old young woman has no life of her own?" Stupid question. Of course Nola didn't think it was sad. She thought it was the way things should be. She *liked* it this way.

"You have a very good life, Elizabeth. You might be more grateful."

That's right, make me feel guilty, Elizabeth thought angrily. That always works. Aloud, she said, "But it's *your* life I'm living, Mother. Why would you want your eighteen-year-old daughter living like a matron? Why would any mother?" Sorry, Max, she apologized silently, I'm borrowing your words. But she knew he wouldn't mind. They were true, after all.

True or not, Nola found them shocking.

"Elizabeth! What a cruel thing to say! As if I haven't always wanted the very best for you." She shook her head and although Elizabeth couldn't see them in the darkness, she was sure there were tears trembling on her mother's lashes. "What has got into you suddenly? I thought you were quite content with our life. You seemed to be. It seems to me we've done very well, recovering from our horrible tragedy. Other women we know have not done nearly so well. Maxine Lewis never leaves her house, even though it's been a year since she lost Gregory, and Trudy and Beth Winterthur have yet to return from Europe. They say they couldn't bear to return to the house on Riverside Drive since their father's death at sea. They have no intention of coming back to pick up the pieces as you and I have done."

Joseph brought the car to a halt in the circular driveway.

Elizabeth sighed again. "*You* have done well, Mother. *You* have picked up the pieces of your life. I, on the other hand, have picked up those very same pieces." She sat forward on the seat. "But they aren't *mine*. At least, they shouldn't be. I should have my own. It's time I started finding them, don't you think?" She could have sworn she saw Joseph's black chauffeur's cap nodding agreement in the front seat. But she couldn't have. He wouldn't dare, not with Nola sitting right behind him. Joseph knew who signed his weekly paycheck. It wasn't Elizabeth.

To her dismay, she was right about the discussion ending when they entered the house. Nola dropped her fur stole on a chair and went directly upstairs to bed without another word, not even a "good night."

Instead of following her mother up the stairs, Elizabeth went into the drawing room and straight to the desk where the telephone sat. She perched on her father's enormous mahogany desk while she dialed the number, then she crossed her legs and waited, one ear attuned to any sound of her mother returning downstairs, the other glued to the receiver, waiting for Max's voice.

When it came, the knot in her stomach melted. His voice always did that, always had, from the first night on board the ship, after that humiliating encounter in the dining room, when he'd come up behind her on the *Titanic* to say teasingly, "Helped any more third-class passengers since I saw you last?"

"I had an argument with my mother tonight," she told him, keeping her voice low. "About my future. I told her I'm not going to Atlantic City in July." Max hadn't wanted her to go away this summer. He wasn't going to Atlantic City with his parents, though they'd thawed enough to invite him. He wanted Elizabeth to stay in the city with him. She had said she couldn't do that. But . . . maybe she could. Maybe she *should*. Be proud of me, Max, Elizabeth pleaded silently. Understand how hard this is for me, because I keep hearing my father's voice telling me to take care of my mother.

But when Max spoke, it was to ask, "Did you mean it? Are you going to stick to it? Or will she get round you, like she always does?"

Elizabeth sagged in disappointment. He didn't trust her. He had no faith left in her. She needed his support now more than ever, and he wasn't going to give it. Maybe she shouldn't have expected him to, after all the times she'd disappointed him this past year. She forged on, "I meant it. I'm not going. I have to think of a way that I can go to college without breaking my promise to my father. There must be something . . . at any rate, I need the summer to think about it. So I can't take any trips."

This brought the reaction she'd hoped for. "Well, good for you! Is the old Elizabeth back then? About time." Max laughed. "I've missed you."

Elizabeth smiled, warmed by his enthusiasm. "Me too."

"Tell you what. You can prove you mean it by meeting me on Saturday afternoon. We'll picnic in Central Park. I'll get all the food at the deli on the corner. All you have to do is show up. Have Joseph bring you to my place. I'll drive on over to my parents' house tomorrow afternoon and pick up a couple of bicycles. We'll bike to the park."

Elizabeth thought fast. Saturday afternoon ... Saturday ... Nola's hairdresser was coming to the house at ten A.M. sharp, and after that there was a shopping trip to Lord & Taylor. But ... that was for summer resort clothes. Since she wasn't going to any resort this summer, what did she need with resort clothes? "Mother will be keeping Joseph busy. But I can take a taxi. I'll be there." If her voice quavered just a bit at the thought of openly defying her mother for the first time in a year, Max didn't comment on it. "What if it rains?"

Max laughed again. "It wouldn't dare." His voice softened then. "Elizabeth, I'm glad you're back. I've missed you a lot. We can have a great summer."

It was nice to hear Max so excited. He'd seemed so unhappy lately. Or maybe "intense" was a better word. Not the carefree, confident Max she'd known on the ship. But then, she hadn't been herself lately, either. She didn't even know who her "self" was anymore.

That would all change now. If she just stuck to her guns and didn't let Nola's theatrics change her mind. Because Max was right. No matter what her father had asked of her on the *Titanic* on that last, terrible night, he would *not* demand that she live her mother's life. That would be too cruel. Her father had not been cruel.

"I'll see you on Saturday," she said into the telephone. "And Max? I love you."

"I love you, too, Elizabeth." He sounded in better spirits than he had in a long time. In a year, perhaps.

Now all she had to do was show up on Saturday, in spite of her mother's best efforts to drag her on yet another shopping foray.

Feeling more hopeful than she had in a very long time, Elizabeth went upstairs.

# Chapter 8

"You will do no such thing." Nola's voice was firm, leaving no room for argument. "Joseph has the car ready. When Tessie has finished with my hair, we are going shopping, Elizabeth."

Tessie, a small, dark-haired woman whose nimble fingers were arranging Nola's thick, fair hair, tightened her lips in disapproval as Elizabeth began arguing with her mother. "I promised Max! And I'm keeping my promise. Haven't you always said a lady should never break her word?"

"You had no business making such a promise in the first place. You knew we had this shopping trip planned."

Elizabeth threw up her hands. "We *always* have a shopping trip planned. Most of our lives are spent shopping! We spend more time in Lord & Taylor than we do at home. Why don't we just set up cots there so we don't have to go home when they close?"

Tessie, who had four children of her own, clucked her tongue, shook her head, the message being, If any of my children were to talk to me that way. . . .

Elizabeth ignored her. "I'm *going* on a picnic with Max. I'm going to have some fun for a change. I'm not an old lady and I'm not going to live like one."

Tessie gasped in shock, and Nola's beautiful face went bone-white. Elizabeth had scored a direct hit on her mother's vanity.

Realizing her mistake, she floundered. "I . . . I didn't mean you were *old*, Mother, you're not, of course you're not, everyone says how young you look. I just meant . . . all those ladies who go shopping every afternoon and then meet later for ice cream sodas, well, they're all *married*, and have children. I . . . I feel out of place with them, that's all I meant."

"My friends are not *old*, Elizabeth," an only slightly mollified Nola said coldly. "And you know perfectly well we do more than just shop. We spend a great deal of time doing charity work. We care about the unfortunate poor. And some of us have been very active in establishing memorials to the victims of the *Titanic*."

Elizabeth frowned. What did any of that have to do with a picnic in the park? Max was waiting for her. If she disappointed him again. . . . "I'm going, Mother. I don't want to be late. Max already thinks you'll change my mind for me. If I don't show up on time, he'll go on without me."

Nola's demeanor changed suddenly. She sagged in the pink upholstered chair, her head went down, and her voice lowered to almost a whisper. "What would your father say, Elizabeth, if he saw you defying me like this?"

Elizabeth had been prepared for this familiar tactic. Nola used it when all else failed. "He would suggest that you go shopping with Betsy and Caroline and let me spend some time with people my own age." She couldn't be positive her father *would* say that, given the instructions he'd delivered only moments before she and her mother climbed into the lifeboat. "Take care of your mother," he had said. But he couldn't possibly have meant that she should spend every waking minute at her mother's side. Surely he wouldn't mind if she took a brief holiday on a sunny Saturday afternoon. Once in a whole year? That wasn't so terrible, was it? "Father would see that as fair, and you know it, Mother."

Her spine straight as a flagpole, Elizabeth headed for the door. Inside, she was shaking, but aloud she said, "Have a good time shopping,

Mother. I'll look forward to seeing all your purchases when I get home this afternoon. Buy something in sapphire blue. It's your best color." There! Now if her mother should suddenly die in a traffic accident while her disobedient, disrespectful daughter was out picnicking in Central Park, at least their last words hadn't been hateful ones.

"Elizabeth!"

Elizabeth was careful to close the door quietly behind her.

"I knew you'd make it!" Max cried when she stepped out of the taxicab. He was sitting on the steps of his building, dressed casually in slacks and a white sweater, a wicker picnic basket beside him. Two bicycles were propped against the steps. Max always looked more handsome when he was happy, and he was happy now. His deep blue eyes glowed with warmth. "I knew you wouldn't back down."

"No, you didn't," Elizabeth replied calmly, smiling and reaching out to take his hand. "You thought I'd give in. But here I am. And you look happy to see me. I like that."

"I'm always glad to see you. I just wish I saw you more often."

"You've been busy, too, Max," she reminded him. "I'm so anxious to see your new work. Couldn't I see it now, while I'm here?"

"Nothing's ready yet, Elizabeth. Won't be for quite a while. I've got this new idea . . . well, I figure, maybe around Christmastime?"

"Christmas! That's months away! I can't wait that long."

Max shrugged. "Sorry. I'm working as fast as I can, but it's got to be right. It's all got to be just right, and that takes time." He balanced the picnic basket on the handlebars of one of the bicycles, strapping it in place with ropes. "Can you stay for the evening? Some of us are going to the roof garden at the Victoria. They have a trained monkey, you know, and singing waiters. It might be fun. Give you a chance to see another side of New York life."

Elizabeth knew about the rooftop restaurant at the Victoria. Her mother thought it "vulgar," and would be horrified if she knew Elizabeth had actually gone there. "I don't see how I can make my mother any angrier than she already is, so perhaps I will go." Glancing down at her white middy and navy blue knife-pleated skirt, she asked, "Can I go dressed like this? I have no evening clothes with me."

Max cared little about clothes. He shrugged. "You can wear whatever you want. Anne won't be dressed up. She never is."

Elizabeth nodded. A large, plain girl, Anne often dressed in suits, bought at thrift shops, claiming they were more comfortable than "stupid hobbled skirts which make it impossible to walk freely."

"I'll go to the Victoria, then. But I don't want to worry my mother, so I'll have to be home by ten." She would deal with Nola's anger then.

They had a wonderful time in Central Park. When they had tired of riding, Max spread an old but clean blanket in an uncrowded, grassy spot, where they ate a delicious lunch of cold chicken and potato salad, topped off with thick slices of chocolate cake. While they ate, they watched people playing lawn tennis, walking their dogs, bicycling by, and Elizabeth marveled, as she always did, at the sheer number of people who frequented the enormous, beautiful park in the heart of the city. It was a wonder to her that this valuable piece of real estate had never been sold to a developer to put up yet another cluster of skyscrapers. She hoped it never would be, but that seemed unlikely.

Max had brought along a ball. They played catch in the sunshine for nearly an hour. Elizabeth could feel the sun's heat on her face, and knew Nola would remark on it first thing. "You might at least have worn a hat to protect your fair skin from sunburn," she would say. That is, if she spoke to her daughter at all.

When they were resting on the blanket following their game of catch, Max asked, "You're not feeling bad, are you? About deserting your mother, I mean?"

"We were just going shopping, Max. It isn't as if we had dinner plans or tickets to the opera. I am so tired of shopping, and I told her that."

Max traced the outline of her cheek with one finger. His eyes were very tender, his smile sweet. "You stood up to her to be with me. I can't tell you how good that makes me feel, Elizabeth. And you were right, I *wasn't* sure you would come today. You've been so different lately. Ever since we came back. . . ."

Elizabeth put a finger against his lips. "Shh! I don't want to talk about coming back, because if we do, then we might end up talking about what we came back *from*, and I don't want to do that. Not today. I *do* want to, sometime. Just not today, all right? Let's just pretend we met right here, in New York, maybe even here in the park. Wouldn't that be fun? We could pretend we just met, right here, today."

Max shook his head solemnly. "Oh, no, we can't pretend that. Because if we'd just met, I couldn't do this. It wouldn't be proper." And he leaned over and kissed her.

To Elizabeth it was the sweetest kiss they'd shared in a long while. The beauty of the park, the sun warming her clear through to her bones, the budding trees, the clear blue sky overhead, and Max holding her, all combined to make the afternoon so pleasurable, she was willing to take whatever the consequences might be for her defiance. She was feeling happy again and young again, and loved again.

As their lips parted, Elizabeth laughed softly.

"What's funny?" Max began packing the picnic basket, a sign that he was ready to leave.

"I was just thinking, if my mother had seen that kiss, she would add 'a public display of affection' to my list of offenses, and I wouldn't be allowed to leave the house again until I was forty-five years old. Maybe fifty. She detests public displays of affection."

Max glanced around. "There are other couples kissing."

Elizabeth laughed again. "Yes, but those young women are not related to my mother."

When they had rested a while from their bicycle ride back to Max's apartment building, they set out to meet Anne, Bledsoe, and Max's friend Gregory at the Victoria. She couldn't wait to tell Anne she'd decided to stay in the city for the summer, and apply to college. Anne wouldn't believe her, of course. "You and your mother are going to grow old together," she'd said one afternoon when they were browsing in the library. "Doesn't that make your blood run cold?"

Elizabeth almost answered, "But, Anne, my blood always runs cold. It has for nearly a year now."

Now, holding Max's hand in hers, walking to his car, Elizabeth felt lighter of heart than she had in a very long time. I wish I lived here in Greenwich Village, too, she was thinking. There is so much going on here. Even in late evening, the Village streets were busy with people. Twilight cast a pale purplish glow over the budding trees and the red and brown brick buildings. On Murray Hill, the streets would be hushed and deserted as families prepared for their evening meal. But here, the streets were as crowded as at midday.

Elizabeth continued to daydream. I would like to have my own little apartment, like Max, and walk to the store on the corner to buy food for my dinner, and maybe have a nice job teaching school or as a secretary. To have my own money, my own home, to be independent and not have to go clothes shopping every day of my life, that would be heaven. She had read about secretaries in *Collier's* magazine. She would live in her own apartment, probably a walk-up, and work in a nice office in one of the tall buildings. On weekday mornings, she would get up and dress for work in a simple suit, water the plants on her windowsill, eat an egg or a biscuit with her coffee, then run to catch a trolley car or perhaps the subway to her office building. She would lunch at Child's with the other girls, and once a week they would all go to the movies after work, and maybe to the Automat for dinner. One article she had read mentioned how tasty the Automat's raisin pie was. She had never had raisin pie.

But, she thought soberly, before I can get a job of any sort, I need to know how to *do* something for which someone would be willing to pay me. I need to know *more*. I need to go to college.

If she didn't get to Vassar, she could go to the City College of New York. CCNY wasn't as expensive as Vassar, that much she knew. If she worked and saved her money, perhaps she could afford a few classes there.

But what would she do about Nola? "Take care of your mother. . . ."

Unwilling to ruin the lovely afternoon by wishing for what she didn't yet have and wasn't sure she ever would, Elizabeth put all thoughts of college out of her head and concentrated on the pleasant time at hand.

She would deal with her mother when she got home.

# Chapter 9

Bledsoe and Anne were waiting for Max and Elizabeth in front of the Victoria. He looked splendid, if a bit theatrical, in a long, black cape and aviator spectacles. Anne was dressed in a brown suit and black bowler hat. They looked to Elizabeth as if they had just come from performing in a play on Broadway. "So, Betsy," Anne said as Max and Elizabeth joined them, "how'd you get out of your cage? Pick the lock?"

Elizabeth laughed, though she winced at the nickname, which Anne knew perfectly well she hated. It reminded her of Betsy Winslow and her twenty-two place settings of china.

"I hope you like this place," Bledsoe said to Elizabeth. "I don't think it's what you're accustomed to."

"Then I'm certain I'll like it," Elizabeth said, laughing lightly.

And she did. And it *wasn't* what she was accustomed to. Nola would have loathed it. It was noisy and merry and very entertaining. The singing waiters actually knew how to sing, the trained monkey was adorable although Elizabeth couldn't help wincing just a bit when he landed on a table where people were eating, the music, much of it ragtime, very upbeat. It was very like a New Year's Eve party . . . but not among her mother's crowd . . . much more fun than that.

The best part was dancing with Max. She hadn't danced with him since the *Titanic*. The annual Farr Christmas party last year had of course been cancelled, so there'd been no dancing over the holidays. It was wonderful to be in his arms, and at some point, Elizabeth smiled up at him and said, "I'm not cold."

He didn't hear her over the noise of music and laughter and feet pounding around the dance floor. He bent his head. "What?"

"I'm not cold!" she shouted in his ear. "Maybe it's because there are so many people in here, or maybe it's because we've been dancing so much, but I'm warm down to my bones for the first time in . . . in a very long time."

Max grinned. "Maybe it's because your bones know you're taking them off to college."

"I don't know that yet, Max," she cautioned. "I said I have to come up with an *idea*. A way to get there without breaking my promise to my father. And if you ask me," she added, faking a pout, "you don't seem at all unhappy over the prospect of me going away. Aren't you going to miss me?"

He pulled her closer. "Am I ever! But you're not going to be that far away. I'll drive up to see you, and you'll be home on weekends, won't you? You won't have to spend every minute with your mother, will you?"

"My mother," Elizabeth said, resting her cheek on his shoulder, "probably won't be speaking to me." Reminded that she still had her mother's wrath to face when she got home, she asked Max what time it was. He stopped dancing and pulled out his pocket watch. Elizabeth gasped. "Ten o'clock? How did it get so late? Oh, Max, I have to go. She's already furious with me."

He understood. "I'm just glad we had such a grand day," he said as he drove her home. "I wish we could do this more often."

If I lived in the Village, we could, Elizabeth thought. But living in the Village would have to wait until she'd finished school. Then, maybe . . .

When Max had parked in front of the Farr house, they were both unwilling to see the day end. They sat in the car so long, Elizabeth was surprised that her mother didn't come rushing out of the house to drag her inside. "I could come in with you," Max offered. "Defend you, like a knight in shining armor."

Elizabeth laughed. "That's so sweet. But I'll survive, I promise. I'll telephone you tomorrow and let you know how bad it was."

They parted reluctantly, with one last, satisfying kiss to get them through the night . . . and to give Elizabeth added courage.

Then, taking a deep breath and letting it out, she went up the steps and into the house.

She was fully prepared to confront an angry parent. What she was *not* prepared for was the sight of Alan Reed, her former fiancé, chatting away in the parlor with Nola, who looked far from angry. Instead, when Elizabeth appeared in the doorway, her mother smiled. "Well, here she is! Look who's come to call, Elizabeth, isn't this lovely? Alan was just in the neighborhood. He was wondering how we were and decided to pay us a visit! And you'll never guess, dear, he's agreed to go with us to Atlantic City!" Suddenly aware of Elizabeth's appearance, she frowned and added, "Well, my goodness, Elizabeth, what *have* you been up to? Your hair . . . and there are grass stains on your skirt."

Elizabeth remained in the doorway. She barely nodded a greeting to Alan, who stood beside the fireplace, a china cup in his hand. "I went on a picnic, Mother. You get grass stains on a picnic." If she knew about the kiss in the park, grass stains would seem trivial in comparison.

And did Nola really think her daughter so stupid that she'd believe Alan was just "in the neighborhood"? He had been *summoned*. That was clear. And to invite him along on their summer vacation! How dare she!

And had she forgotten, or was she just ignoring, Elizabeth's vow not to leave the city this summer? "I'm not going, Mother. Did you forget?"

"Of course you're going. Elizabeth, you have never spent a summer in the city. You don't know how intolerable the heat becomes. *No one* stays here during the hottest months. The city is deserted."

It was true, Elizabeth had never spent a summer in the city. Ever since she was a small child, the Farrs, along with everyone else they knew, had summered at the seashore in Atlantic City, or on Long Island Sound at their summer house, or in the Catskills, where it was always cooler. Nola had sold the summer house last year, saying she couldn't bear to visit there, with so many "memories of Martin." But there were numerous invitations from friends who had homes on the Sound, if they chose to go there.

Elizabeth knew that New York, at least in

her neighborhood, was virtually a cemetery during the hottest months. All of her friends would be away. Not that she saw them that often anymore, what with spending so much time with her mother. Most of the girls she'd gone to school with were engaged now and busy planning their weddings.

Elizabeth moved on into the room and sank into one of the white velvet chairs flanking the fireplace. Alan, who had lost a bit more hair and gained a few more pounds, looked no more attractive to her than he ever had. But when he smiled his banker's smile at her, she returned the smile because it seemed petty not to. It wasn't Alan's fault that Nola manipulated people as if they were figures on a chessboard. And he was a decent sort, though no more interesting than the chessboard itself. Elizabeth would have felt worse about breaking the engagement had Alan accepted the news differently. He had simply nodded and drawn on his pipe, as if she had said, "It's not going to rain tomorrow" instead of "I'm not going to marry you, Alan."

Later, Nola had excused his lack of reaction by explaining, "He knew you were grieving for your father, Elizabeth. Alan is much too considerate to put his own needs ahead of yours."

Elizabeth had raised an eyebrow. The only needs Alan Reed seemed to have, as far as she had ever seen, were eating, smoking his pipe, and riding horses. She truly believed that if one of his horses died he'd have far more emotional a reaction than he'd had upon learning that Elizabeth Farr wasn't going to marry him.

So what was he *doing* here, after all this time?

Nola began prattling on about the upcoming vacations. There would be three trips. The first of these would take them to Alan's country house in Tarrytown, for two weeks. He had been kind enough to invite them. . . .

As she talked, Elizabeth closed her eyes. Every time she thought she had regained some of what she'd lost when the ship sank, something happened to prove her wrong. Today she had defied her mother and refused to go shopping. That had felt wonderful. And the picnic had been wonderful as well. But tonight, her mother was planning a summer vacation for both of them.

". . . And a new riding outfit, Elizabeth, you simply must have one this year. Alan tells me he has a new thoroughbred you're going to love. . . ."

"You'll take care of your mother?" her father had said during those last painful moments on board the *Titanic*. He had known, then, that he would not be leaving with his wife and daughter. He had to have been frightened, terrified.

But the only feelings he'd expressed to Elizabeth were his concerns for his family. Especially his wife. "You must promise me, Elizabeth. You and your mother will be taken care of financially, but she will need much more than that. You must stay with her and care for her. And if you marry, you must take her to live with you."

Elizabeth had promised, even though her father's request sounded like a life sentence. It also sounded unnecessary. Martin Farr may not have recognized his wife's inner strength, but Elizabeth did. She had seen it for herself more than once. Her mother was perfectly capable of managing her own life. The difficulty was, she didn't *want* to. Independence held no appeal for her at all. She considered it "unladylike." "Why aren't those women home tending to their children and husbands?' she queried upon reading of a suffrage march or rally in the morning newspaper. "Perhaps no one would marry them. That would explain their shrillness, wouldn't it?"

"My cousin Candace is being married in July," Alan said, interrupting Elizabeth's depressing thoughts. "I do hope you'll both attend."

Nola looked up with interest. "Candace? Isn't she the cousin who lost her husband to influenza? She's been widowed for what, three years now?"

"Three and a half. With two young children to look after. She's had a rather difficult time of it. This new fellow is much older, nearing fifty, I believe. But he's a good sort and Candace will be relieved of much of her burden."

"That's a stupid reason for marrying," Elizabeth remarked.

Her mother and her former fiancé looked at her as if to say, Is there a better reason?

And that was when the idea sprang, full-blown, into Elizabeth's head.

There *was* a way to escape. There was a way to fulfill her promise to her father and still have her independence. All she had to do . . . why hadn't she thought of it before . . . all she had to do was find Nola a *husband*!

She wouldn't be betraying her father. He wouldn't mind. He wanted his wife taken care of. He wouldn't be angry if it was by a husband instead of a daughter.

It shouldn't be all that difficult, finding someone. Nola was young, not yet forty, and very beautiful, with gentility, breeding, and character. Any intelligent man with taste would be thrilled to have such a woman.

Of course, it couldn't be just *any* man. The first requisite was, he would have to be wealthy. Nola would expect . . . no, demand, to be pampered in a new marriage just as she had been in her first. She had her own money, plenty of it, but at the rate she was spending it, it wouldn't hurt to have another income handy. Wealth was definitely an important consideration when seeking a new husband for Nola Farr.

So . . . wealth and generosity were requirements. Also character, as she had no wish to see her mother with a scoundrel, and there were plenty of those about, according to newspaper accounts. Wealth, generosity, and character . . . that might do it.

Where might Elizabeth find such a man?

Didn't Alan have an uncle who was a bachelor? He'd be wealthy, of course. Alan would never tolerate a poor relation. And he spoke kindly of this uncle, so the man couldn't be poor. Cedric, wasn't that his name? Uncle Cedric, he of the large estate in Tarrytown-on-the-Hudson, not far from Alan's country house.

Of course, the man would most likely also be dull, like his nephew, and probably not nearly as good-looking as Martin Farr. But hadn't Nola herself just put her stamp of approval on the "sensible" marriage of Alan's widowed cousin? She hadn't said a word about the prospective groom's appearance or personality. If those things shouldn't matter to the cousin, they should be of no importance to Nola, as well.

For the first time in months, she felt something stirring within her. She couldn't be sure what it was, didn't recognize the feeling. Excitement? Hope, maybe? Whatever it was, it was good to feel *something*.

She could hardly wait to share her new plan with Max. Perhaps his father knew someone suitable.

Meanwhile, she would go with her mother to Tarrytown and arrange a meeting between Nola and Alan's bachelor-uncle Cedric or Chester or whatever it was. Perhaps it was Cecil.

Elizabeth lifted her head. "I think," she said slowly, as if she were waking from a long sleep, "that a new riding outfit would be a good idea. My jacket from last year has a hole in the elbow from a fall."

Nola beamed at her daughter with approval.

"By the way, Alan," Elizabeth asked later as her former fiancé was taking his leave, "what was the name of that uncle you're so fond of, the one who lives near your Tarrytown house? If I remember correctly, he grows award-winning tomatoes." Nola had retired for the night and was safely out of hearing.

Though the night was warm, Alan carefully wrapped a white silk muffler about his neck. "You must be speaking of Casper. My uncle Casper."

"Yes, of course." Her eyes innocent, Elizabeth asked, "Is he still single?"

Alan sighed. "He is. We Reed men seem to be devilishly unlucky in matters of the heart."

Refusing to rise to the bait, Elizabeth asked, "And does he still live in Tarrytown?"

"Of course. His estate is one of the most impressive in the area."

Elizabeth mentally checked off "wealthy" on her list. Looks and personality were something else again. But she was willing to take things one step at a time, now that she had an idea. Now that she had a plan. Now that she had hope.

Perhaps, with luck and timing and perseverance, the dreams she'd had before the *Titanic* disaster could be resurrected after all.

# Chapter 10

"You're *not* going!" Max said flatly when Elizabeth explained over the telephone, in hushed tones, her plan. He couldn't believe she was planning on spending two weeks at Alan's country house in Tarrytown-on-the-Hudson. "First off, your mother isn't going to let someone pick out a fellow for her. Second, if you think I'm going to shout hooray at the idea of you spending two weeks in the company of your former fiancé, think again!"

"I never agreed to be engaged to him," Elizabeth reminded him, keeping her voice calm. "That was all my parents' doing, Max, and you know it. So what are you worried about? You know I never loved Alan." She smiled into the telephone. "You're worried that a sudden, mad passion for Alan Reed will overtake me and I'll throw myself into his arms with abandon?"

"Something like that," Max admitted grudgingly. "It isn't really you I don't trust. It's your mother. She always gets what she wants. And what she wants is for you to give me the old heave-ho and marry Alan Reed, which is why he suddenly showed up tonight at your house. You *know* she invited him, probably because you defied her today and spent the afternoon with me. That must have really worried her."

"She doesn't *always* get what she wants," Elizabeth reminded him.

He knew immediately what she meant. "You're right. I'm sorry. That was thoughtless of me. But when it comes to you, she does. At least, ever since..." He paused, then went ahead and said it, "Ever since we got back."

Elizabeth didn't want to argue with Max. She'd be leaving the city soon, leaving *him*, and it was important that they part on good terms. "I have to do this, Max. If I can find someone to take care of her, I'll be free of my promise to my father. I can apply to Vassar the very second I know she's going to be in good hands."

Max made a rude sound. "As if the woman isn't perfectly capable of taking care of herself. Look at the way she runs that house. At the way she runs *you*...."

Elizabeth sighed. "I know. But she doesn't *want* to take care of herself." She sighed again. "I just hope Alan's wealthy Uncle Casper is at least reasonably good-looking."

He wasn't. Alan's wealthy Uncle Casper was an older replica of Alan. Meeting the man, seeing uncle and nephew side by side, Elizabeth felt as if she were viewing two photographs of the same man, except that one of them had been taken twenty years after the first. The resemblance was uncanny . . . and dispiriting. Martin Farr had been so handsome. It was hard to imagine her beautiful mother on the arm of someone like Casper Reed, who had lost a bit more hair than his nephew and bore a few more pounds around the middle. How could Nola ever be attracted to Casper Reed?

But, Elizabeth reminded herself sternly to lift her sagging spirits, if Alan, a younger version of Casper in every way, was good enough for *me* in Nola's eyes, why shouldn't the older version of him be acceptable to *her*?

She realized the flaw in that logic instantly. Alan had only been acceptable in her *parents'* eyes . . . never in hers. She herself had never been attracted to him. How likely then was it that Nola would be attracted to his uncle? Nevertheless, it was worth a try. Elizabeth hadn't made the trip from Manhattan to Tarrytown to give up so easily.

Nola did seem happy to be in the country again. And Casper's estate was impressive. Acre upon acre of lush green land, in the middle of which sat an enormous stone and frame dwelling twice the size of Alan's house. If Elizabeth was less impressed by the lack of imagination in the decorating of the bachelor's home, she assured herself that Nola could remedy that easily enough. If she chose to.

She did *not* choose to. After five days and evenings spent in the company of nephew and uncle, Nola was ready to go home.

"The days are entertaining enough," she confided to Elizabeth as she prepared for bed on a warm summer evening in July. "But the evenings!" Nola sighed. "One more night of conversation about dogs and horses, hunting and banking, and I think I shall go mad."

Thoroughly disheartened by her mother's clear lack of interest in Casper Reed as a suitor, Elizabeth argued, "Mother, dinner conversation among your friends is hardly more stimulating." She had thrown Nola and Casper together at every opportunity, suffering through long, tedious hours alone with Alan, hoping some spark would flare up between the two adults. It hadn't. Though Casper seemed intrigued by his beautiful companion, it was clear that Nola was no more attracted to him than to the stone fence guarding the man's property.

"You could have been friendlier to Casper.

He's very wealthy, you know," Elizabeth said. "And he's not a bad sort. He seems very taken with *you*."

Nola gasped. Her jaw dropped in an unlady-like gape. "Casper? As a suitor? For *me*? Oh, Elizabeth, you can't be serious! You were actually entertaining such a ridiculous notion? Why, the man is nothing like your father. Even if I *were* thinking along such lines, now that my period of mourning is over, and I assure you I am *not*, Casper Reed would certainly not be a candidate." She paused, thought for a minute or two, then her eyes narrowed. "Elizabeth? Is that why you were willing to come up here? You were . . . you were thinking that Casper and I . . ." Nola broke off in mid-sentence to laugh. At first it was just a small, ladylike laugh. But as she continued dwelling on Elizabeth's intention, her laugh gained strength and momentum, until it rang out in the room like a chorus of bells. She bent double at the waist, laughing and gasping at the same time.

After several long minutes, Nola wiped her eyes, gasping, "Casper Reed! Oh, Elizabeth . . ."

"Why wouldn't Casper be a candidate, Mother?" Elizabeth asked when Nola had regained control. "Because he's too much like his nephew? Too dull, too boring, and not at all handsome?" She kept her voice very quiet, aware of Alan sleeping somewhere on the same floor. "Yet you found Alan perfectly acceptable for *me*."

Nola frowned. She wiped her eyes with a linen handkerchief. "That is very different."

"How is it different?" Elizabeth picked up a magazine and waved it for emphasis. "Your daughter doesn't deserve a handsome, interesting husband but you *do*? Isn't that terribly hypocritical, Mother?"

Nola faced her dressing table mirror and started brushing her hair. "Nonsense. You're young. You need the stability of someone like Alan, who can establish a respectable, secure life for you. I, on the other hand, already have an adequate income, my own home, an established life. Your father saw to that."

Elizabeth mulled that over. Then she said, "So, what you're saying is, you have everything you need. You don't need Casper. You don't need a husband. You don't need *anyone* to take care of you. Isn't that what you're saying?"

Realizing the trap she had fallen into, Nola hastened to repair the damage. "Not as long as I have *you*, dear. What would I need with a husband when I have my darling daughter at my side?"

But it was too late. Much too late. The first mistake Nola had made was laughing at her daughter. The second mistake was insisting that her life was well-ordered. That she didn't need a husband to care for her. Elizabeth had always known this was true, though her father hadn't seen it. But she had never before heard her mother admit it.

All right, then. She would apply to Vassar College. And she would be accepted, she was certain of that. She would take the train home every weekend to make sure her mother was doing well, and to see Max. But she *would* be leaving the house in Murray Hill.

Because her mother was fine, *would* be fine. Hadn't she just said so herself?

Sensing that something was happening but unable to figure out exactly what it was, Nola turned once again on the vanity stool. She glanced at the magazine in Elizabeth's hand, and anxious for a diversion, said as if nothing out of the ordinary had taken place, "Oh, darling, look at the gorgeous green hat on the cover! Do look inside the magazine and see if it tells us where I might find that hat. It would go so beautifully with my green suit, the one with the ermine collar."

Elizabeth smiled. "Oh, it would, Mother, you're right." Still smiling, she began leafing through the magazine again. Though she appeared to be searching the pages for information about where her mother might purchase the green hat on the cover, she was actually mentally composing her letter of inquiry to Vassar about admissions policies.

*Dear Sir or Madam,*

*You will be happy to hear (though not nearly as happy as I was) that my mother is perfectly satisfied with her life, perfectly capable of caring for herself and therefore I am writing to inquire how I might become a matriculating student at your fine establishment . . .*

or:

*Dear Sir or Madam,*

*Might you have room at your fine establishment for a young woman who has had enough shopping on Fifth Avenue to last her a full lifetime?*

"Have you found it yet?" Nola asked.

"No. But I'm still looking."

They returned to New York the following day, a sticky, sultry, Thursday afternoon in mid-July.

A month before Elizabeth had secretly written to Vassar College, applying for admission. She had asked for a scholarship, saying she wanted to be independent of her family. She doubted, at the time, she would be able to leave her mother, but she wanted to have hope.

On a Tuesday morning, she received her acceptance letter. *"We are pleased to inform you...."* Not only had she been accepted, but because of her "excellent academic standing" in her "lower-form education," she was being offered a scholarship that would meet most of her expenses.

Elizabeth couldn't believe her good fortune. Now, even if her mother disapproved, she would be able to go. She could get a part-time job in Poughkeepsie, perhaps as a salesclerk in a department store, to cover the remainder of her expenses.

The first person she shared this joyful news with was Max, by telephone. He was as elated as she was. When she had returned from Tarrytown and shared with him what had happened there, how her decision to apply to college had come about, he'd been almost as excited as she was. But he reminded her that because she had applied so late, she would have to tell her mother right away.

She did.

Upon hearing the news, Nola collapsed.

# Chapter 11

"Well, of course you can't possibly go," Nola said flatly when Elizabeth, her stomach churning, had read aloud the contents of her letter from Vassar. "I can't imagine what you were thinking, applying to college behind my back and not even discussing it with me first."

They were outside, in the garden, where Elizabeth had found her mother gathering a bouquet of pink roses. She would have done almost anything to avoid this confrontation. But she was to leave for Poughkeepsie soon. Perhaps Max would drive her. If not, she could take the train. At any rate, there was not enough time to break the news gently to her mother.

"I didn't discuss it with you," Elizabeth said, "because I wasn't sure I'd be accepted. But now I have been, and I *am* going, Mother. They've given me a scholarship. I won't turn that down."

Nola tilted her head, protected from the sun by a wide-brimmed straw hat. "You're *not* going, Elizabeth. I need you here. I can't possibly manage here all by myself."

Elizabeth clutched the sheet of paper in her hands so tightly the fine linen stationery crackled like kernels of corn popping. Nola glanced around as if trying to locate the source of the annoying sound. "You said you didn't need a husband, Mother, remember? At Alan's. You said your life was just fine without a man to take care of you. You *laughed* at my efforts at matchmaking. If you can manage without a husband, why can't you manage without a daughter? You have friends. You have a social life, you said so yourself. You can do the same things with Betsy and Caroline and your other friends that you and I do together. And the household staff will take care of everything else."

"Caroline and Betsy won't be here in the evenings."

"They'd come if you invited them."

Nola's face was quite pale. "It's during the evening that I miss your father most, Elizabeth. He wouldn't want me to be alone then, Elizabeth. He was counting on you to save me from such loneliness."

Elizabeth winced. But she recovered instantly. Nola didn't usually play her trump card . . . Elizabeth's father . . . so quickly. She knows how determined I am this time, Elizabeth guessed, and it's making her desperate. "You could sell the house, Mother, if it's too much for you," she suggested. "You could buy a nice country house, perhaps near some of your Connecticut friends. Or you could take an apartment in the city."

Nola looked horrified. "An apartment?"

"Mother, there are places on Central Park West that are enormous. Some of them are two whole floors, no different than a house." Elizabeth had never seen such places for herself, but Anne and Bledsoe had mentioned them as evidence of the extravagances of the wealthy, when the poor were suffering so.

"If they're no different than a house," Nola responded sharply, "what would be the point of moving? I already *have* a house. And," she added, turning away from Elizabeth to snip one last pale pink rose from its bush, "I'm not leaving it. There are memories of your father here. Nor are you leaving." Carefully placing the flower in the basket she carried over one arm, Nola turned and began walking up the stone path toward the kitchen door.

"I *am* going, Mother!" Elizabeth called after her. "I've been accepted and I'm going. Max is driving me to Poughkeepsie on August twenty-seventh. You'll be fine here. You don't need me.

I'll come home every weekend to spend it with you, but I *am* going."

Afterwards, Elizabeth was never sure of the exact sequence of events. When it played out in her mind later, it was all a confused jumble, as if someone had taken a movie reel, sliced it to pieces, and then spliced it back together all wrong.

But she thought it began when she cried out, "I *am* going!" that last time. Nola stopped on the path, her back to Elizabeth. The basket heaped with pink blossoms dropped to the ground. Nola turned, one hand against her chest, an expression of surprise on her face. She stood like that, motionless, for a second or two, then dropped abruptly to her knees, one hand extending beseechingly toward Elizabeth.

Elizabeth stood frozen, unwillingly to believe what she was seeing. When she could move again, she ran to her mother's side.

"Call Dr. Cooper," Nola whispered with great effort. "Fenton Cooper, *call* him. Hurry!" Then she toppled sideways, landing in Elizabeth's arms.

At the hospital, it seemed to Elizabeth hours, even days, before Dr. Cooper emerged from the emergency room's swinging doors to approach Elizabeth. She was sitting alone on a hard wooden bench in the hallway. The doctor was a handsome man, tall and authoritative, his dark hair graying at the temples. His expression was grim.

Elizabeth jumped to her feet. The ride in the ambulance had been frightening, the suspense while waiting for a diagnosis nerve-wracking. Unable to reach Max by telephone, she had asked Cook to keep calling his number until he answered. Cook hated the telephone, and Elizabeth was afraid she wouldn't do as asked. And now she had to hear what the grim-faced doctor had to say all by herself, instead of having Max at her side. "Is my mother all right?"

"She's doing as well as can be expected." Dr. Cooper motioned Elizabeth to return to the bench, then sat down beside her.

What did *that* mean? "What's wrong with her? What happened? She was fine one minute, then . . . was it the heat? She was wearing a hat against the sun, but . . ."

"Unfortunately," Dr. Cooper said soberly, "a hat is no protection against heart trouble."

Elizabeth's world stopped turning. Every sound in the hospital, every bit of bustling activity among nurses and orderlies, every voiced complaint from emergency room patients awaiting treatment, vanished, disappeared as completely as if Elizabeth had waved a magic wand. She could no longer hear, or speak, or think. The pungent medicinal odor that had been making her head ache was gone. There was nothing left in the hospital but that one phrase: "heart trouble."

Dr. Cooper cleared his throat.

"My mother doesn't have heart trouble," Elizabeth managed, though she had no idea how the words had formed.

"I'm afraid she does."

Not true. Not ... not ... *not* ... true! It couldn't be. Nola had never appeared the slightest bit ill ... no, *that* wasn't true, either. On the ship, on the *Titanic* ... she had been ill. Briefly. But ... that had been seasickness, hadn't it? Many people had it, even though the trip was as smooth as a glide across glass. Smooth until ...

"Is she going to die?"

"Oh, heavens no! I'm sorry if I frightened you, Elizabeth. Her condition is not life-threatening. There is very little treatment, unfortunately, but there *are* ways to keep her out of harm's way. You and I," the doctor said, smiling reassuringly at Elizabeth, "will see to that, won't we? We'll make sure she's well cared for. That's what Martin would expect of us, don't you agree?"

"But ... but she hasn't *seemed* sick," Elizabeth said. She was struggling to comprehend what Dr. Cooper had just told her. "She has so much energy. All those shopping trips ... I get tired long before she does. And her color is good . . . are you positive, Dr. Cooper? That she has this . . . this heart trouble?"

He looked a bit miffed. "Of course I'm sure. I wonder," he added, "if you could tell me what precipitated this spell."

Elizabeth flushed with guilt. She lowered her eyes, studying the black and white floor tiles. "I . . . I told her I was going away to college in August. I'd just been accepted and given a scholarship. She . . . she didn't like the idea."

"Well, of course not. My goodness, Elizabeth, she recently lost her husband. And she finds out her daughter intends to desert her? Why would she like the idea?"

Elizabeth ducked her head further, fighting tears.

"Well," Dr. Cooper said as briskly, patting Elizabeth's hand in an awkward attempt to console her, "no matter now. But it's agreed that we'll have no more talk of you leaving your mother alone in that big house? Your place is, of course, with her." He shook his head. "I myself don't hold with higher education for women. Makes them less content to fulfill their duties in the home when they marry, as most of them do. It gives me chills to think of who might be running the country should women be given the vote."

"Perhaps they would know more about politics," Elizabeth countered, "if they were better educated."

Fenton Cooper had no intention of wasting his valuable time arguing with a stubborn young woman. "About your mother . . . this episode has been very frightening for her. You must reassure her that you'll remain at her side. That will do more to hasten her speedy recovery than any medicine. The important thing, and I must stress this, is that she not be upset or distressed or worried, do you understand that?"

As guilty as Elizabeth was feeling, she had to ask, "Can't you fix it? An operation . . . ?"

"Oh, no, my dear. I'm afraid this is a condition your mother will have to live with. With proper care, of course."

"But she *will* live? This condition, you said it isn't life-threatening, didn't you? Why didn't this happen when she lost my father? She adored him. That had to be the worst thing she's ever gone through. You know how agitated she was, for a long time. But she was never ill."

"That is true. And quite astonishing. I thought so at the time. But your mother is a strong woman, Elizabeth. I believe she tried her best to remain calm for your sake, and it saved her from any cardiac distress. Mothers will do anything to save their children pain. I've seen it many times."

And look how I paid her back, Elizabeth thought, thoroughly ashamed. By planning to leave her.

Standing up, she asked the doctor if she could see her mother. "I won't upset her, I promise."

"Yes, of course. You're just what she needs, I'm sure." Dr. Cooper stood up and led the way down the hall.

They had arrived at the curtain hiding Nola from view. "Remember, now," the doctor cautioned, "she is not to be upset in any way. Comfort and reassurance and a daughter's devotion, that's the ticket. She will be allowed to go home tomorrow morning, where she must rest and remain calm for the remainder of the week. If all goes well, she should be up and about in no time, leading a normal life again for the most part, and this difficult little episode will be behind both of you."

Elizabeth frowned. "A normal life? Even shopping and dinners and parties? But I thought ..."

"She needn't be bedridden. As long as she doesn't become agitated or distressed, she may do as she pleases."

My father's philosophy exactly, Elizabeth couldn't help thinking. Let Nola do as she pleases and don't let anything upset her. What was it about her mother that led men to pamper her so?

Well, a cold, stern voice in her head answered, right *now* it's a heart condition, you spoiled, selfish girl. Your mother fell to her knees in front of you and this is all the compassion you can muster up? Pampered or not, she must have been very frightened.

As *I* was, Elizabeth thought, remembering that terrible moment in the garden.

Thanking the doctor, who then hurried off to attend to other patients, Elizabeth pulled the curtain aside and entered the emergency room cubicle where her mother lay on a bed, her eyes closed.

# Chapter 12

Elizabeth delayed writing to Vassar. All around her in the city, young women were working in office buildings, piloting airplanes, driving automobiles, becoming involved in politics, doing things women had never before done. Once she wrote the letter declining admission, declining the scholarship, her chance of ever having an exciting, interesting life like those other young women would disappear forever.

But if her mother was ill. . . .

"How do you know she's not faking?" Max asked when Elizabeth telephoned him from the hospital.

"Max!"

"Well, I'm sorry, but you have to see how coincidental it is that a perfectly healthy woman collapsed the moment you told her you were going away to college. What better way to keep you from going than to fake an illness?" Max's voice softened. "She had to know you would never leave if she was sick. You're not that kind of daughter."

"The doctor *said* she was sick. It's not as if Nola herself had said it."

"No, I guess not." Max didn't sound convinced. "You're still going to Vassar, though, aren't you? You can hire a nurse for Nola if you think she needs one."

"A nurse? A stranger? Oh, Max, if you could have seen her. . . ." Elizabeth's breath caught in her throat, recalling the sight of her mother on her knees on the stone path. "I honestly thought she was dying. I thought I had killed her. I never should have broken the news to her in that way. Without any preparation. I should have waited for a better time, or dropped little hints that I had applied. Given her some warning."

"You didn't know about her heart."

"Well, I know now."

Following an uncomfortable pause, Max said, "You're not going to go to Vassar. I can hear it in your voice."

From where she stood in the wide, white-walled hallway, Elizabeth had a clear view of her mother's bed. With the curtain pulled partially aside, she could see that Nola's eyes were closed, her face in peaceful repose. "Well . . . not just now. I can't. How can I? Dr. Cooper said Nola could lead an almost-normal life as long as she doesn't become upset or agitated. We both know my leaving would agitate her. Look how upset she got when I told her I'd been accepted. Telling her I was actually *going*, especially now that I know she's ill, would be the undoing of her. I might just as well push her off a cliff."

"So, you're not going," he repeated. He didn't add, I always knew you wouldn't. But Elizabeth heard it, anyway.

"She's *sick*, Max. She's the only parent I have left. Try to understand."

Though it must have taken effort on his part, he became then the Max she had fallen in love with on the *Titanic*. "I do understand, Elizabeth. And I know you have to do what you think is right. Maybe . . . maybe you can go later, when she's better. Or you could take some classes at CCNY. Your mother wouldn't mind that, would she, since you wouldn't be leaving the city?"

Elizabeth felt a rush of warmth for him. He was being so sweet. He wanted her to go to Vassar, he'd always made that clear. And yet here he was, understanding how torn she was feeling, and not pushing her to selfishly abandon her mother . . . who didn't even approve of Max.

\*     \*     \*

Katie's singing career blossomed over the summer months. She sang at parties, lavish weddings, fund-raisers, any celebration that called for entertainment, always in the finest homes, on the grandest estates. The enterprising Flo had raised her fee several times. Each time, Katie feared no one would be willing to pay what she thought of as an astonishing amount of money and her career would end. But that didn't happen. She opened a bank account, began paying Malachy and Lottie a generous rent for her small room, and bought three new gowns of her own choosing. She was careful to keep them simple in design, mindful that Flo had been right about that.

When she wasn't singing or rehearsing, she spent time with Bridget. She and John often took the child to the Brooklyn Pier on a hot Saturday afternoon where, although Bridget was too small to swim in the deep water, she took pleasure in watching the young boys in swim trunks boldly diving in. She would count on her fingers when three or four jumped in at the same time, fearful that they wouldn't all surface. But they always did.

Katie saw less and less of Paddy. When she did see him, he seemed irritable and depressed, and once or twice, she was certain she smelled liquor on his breath. Sensing that the writing of his book for Edmund wasn't going well, she offered to help.

"And when would you be doin' that, pray tell?" he asked. They were walking in Manhattan on a sunny, sultry Saturday afternoon, each armed with a wrapper containing a hot, aromatic sweet potato they'd bought from a street vendor. "Seems to me you've no time now for anything but singin' at those fancy affairs of yours."

Katie recognized envy when she heard it. The good nuns had warned her to steer clear of it. Had they not warned Paddy as well? Not that she blamed him. The tables had turned now. Her dreams were in full flower, while Paddy's were dying on the vine. He struggled so. She had no idea what was getting in his way. She knew only that something was. She wondered if Edmund knew what it was. Or Belle, who was still tutoring Paddy.

Swallowing the last of her sweet potato, Katie tossed the wrapper in a trash can and said, "I'd find time for you, Paddy. Do you not know that? Always, I would find time. If you want."

He shook his head. Reaching out to pat the tangled mane of a sway-backed, emaciated horse waiting at the curb for its master to return to the knife-sharpening cart it pulled, he said,

"Even now you should be home vocalizin', rehearsin' for your engagement tonight. You said so yourself when I called for you at Malachy's."

Such a big mouth she had! She hadn't thought to hurt his feelings when she'd remarked that she should be practicing. But just as Paddy pulled up in front of the rooming-house in a taxicab, Flo had telephoned to remind Katie about her engagement in Larchmont that evening. "Don't you be gadding all over the city getting yourself all worn out," she had warned when Katie said Paddy was taking her into Manhattan. "And get back early enough to warm up those pipes so you'll be in good voice. Going to be some very wealthy, influential people there tonight. You'll be getting some work lined up for the holiday season, is my guess."

The warning about practicing had been so fresh in her mind when Katie ran down the steps and joined Paddy in the taxicab, she'd mentioned the conversation to him. She shouldn't have. It must have sounded to him as if he should think himself fortunate indeed to be in the company of so successful an entertainer.

Which wouldn't be so paining to him, if he was doing as well at his writing.

Not six months ago it was the other way around, Katie thought as she stopped to look in the window of a music equipment store. A beautiful grand piano was on display. Katie was saving up for a piano of her own, though she had no plans to buy anything as fine as the one in the window. A used one would not be so pricey, and would do nicely once it had been properly tuned. Right now, she had to go across the street to Agnes Murphy's to use the piano in the front parlor for her rehearsing. Katie didn't play, but Agnes seemed delighted with the chance to play again.

Agnes's piano was an old relic and could have used the fine hand of a tuner. Katie wanted her own instrument. And she knew if she ever did return to Ireland, she could take the piano, in spite of its size, right along with her. There had been several of them on the *Titanic*. Hadn't she played the one in the third-class common room her own self, while people sang and danced and had a grand time? If steerage had had one piano, second- and third-class decks had probably had more than one. So she wouldn't have to leave a new piano behind should she decide to make the trip home.

John had volunteered to accompany her on the piano if she bought one for their own roominghouse. He missed playing, he said, as he'd done at school and in the church hall back home. But he didn't want to spend the money on a piano as he was, he told her, also saving for a ticket home. Saving up his vacation time at the bank, too. Perhaps, he had suggested one night, talking about Ireland, he and Katie might make the trip together?

She had avoided answering him directly by saying, "Oh, sure and you'll be ready to go long before me. It'll be a while before I can work up me courage to climb aboard a ship again. If I ever can do that. And besides," she had added loyally, "I'd best be waitin' until Paddy's ready to come along with me. Not that I'm sure he ever *will* be." John had made no further comment, but her aunt Lottie had said that night while the two women were drying the dinner dishes, "That boy's sweet on you, any fool could see it. He's a fine Irish lad and he's got himself a good job. You could do worse."

Shocked, Katie had said, "I thought you was fond of Paddy. Are you turnin' on him, then?"

Lottie shook her head. "He's a bright lad, but he ain't got a job, Katie, and no prospects for one as far as I can see. And he'd never settle for you supportin' the both of you, though it seems now like you could. Is he never goin' to write his book?"

Katie had had no answer for that.

"Do you think you'll be buyin' one of them pianos with your singin' money?" Paddy asked as they moved away from the display window.

"I might." Katie, happy to be in the noisy, busy city as long as Paddy was at her side, linked an arm through his. She was wearing one of her new dresses, a simple frock of white dotted swiss with pale yellow ribbon threaded through the hobble and the cuffs and neckline. The skirt was so tight, it was fair strangling her legs, and she had to take smaller steps than she was used to, as if her ankles had been chained together. "But I'm also savin' up for a trip home if I can work up the nerve to climb aboard a ship again. So I mean to be choosy about how much I spend on a piano."

Even as she spoke, the memory of that awful night came back. She felt the cold. She heard the screams, and she trembled.

Paddy shook his head again. He needed a haircut. Katie wondered why Edmund didn't see to it. Didn't Paddy have to look his best when he met all those important people? Maybe it was fine for writers to look like they didn't think about such ordinary things as haircuts. Or . . . was Paddy not meeting with important people these days? Had Edmund given up on him? "Don't know what you'd be goin' back home for," he said. "Ain't nothin' there, nothin' at all."

Katie stopped walking. Since their arms were still linked, Paddy had to stop, too. "My *family* is there, Paddy! Don't you be callin' them nothin'."

"Sorry. Didn't mean that." They began walking again. The streets were crowded with Saturday shoppers, street vendors hawked their wares, and young and middle-aged suffragettes hurried from shop to shop armed with petitions or bearing placards urging the vote for women. Several of them glared at Katie in passing as if they resented the fact that she wasn't helping.

"Maybe," Paddy added, "I'm just worried that you wouldn't come back. I know how you yearn for Ireland and Ballyford. Was you to travel all the way back there, how do I know you wouldn't decide to stay?"

"You could come with me." She smiled up at him. "And talk me out of staying if I'd a mind to. Wouldn't you like to see your ma and da, your granda again, Paddy? Just for a bit?"

Paddy's eyes darkened. "So they could all stand there lookin' at me and wishin' I was Brian? No, thanks."

Katie gasped, stopping abruptly again. "Patrick Kelleher, what a terrible thing to say! They would never wish that!"

"Sure, and I believe they would." His voice was firm, certain.

"You was always the apple of your ma's eyes, Paddy, and that's the truth of it. She'll be pinin' for Bri, like all of us, but 'tis your passin' that would have broke her heart beyond mendin'. She must miss you somethin' fierce. Your da and granda, too. A visit would make them all feel better. Would you just think on it? I mean to go some day. 'Twould be much more pleasant was you to come along with me. And me ma and da would have more peace of heart was I to board a ship with you by my side, and not alone." She was tempted to tell him of John's offer to accompany her. Could be jealousy would do what her pleading would not. But Paddy seemed so disheartened these days, she didn't want to add to his pain, whatever it was.

He laughed bitterly. "Peace of heart? Because of me? 'Twas me brother they trusted you with, Katie, not me."

Even though Katie recognized the truth of that, she hated hearing Paddy being so hard on himself. 'Twasn't like him at all. His old arrogance had ofttimes been maddening, but she'd grown used to it. 'Twas who he was, she'd thought, and loved him just the same.

It had to be the difficulties with his book that was getting him down. Maybe Belle wasn't being as much help as Edmund had thought she would. Katie still didn't understand why Paddy let Belle help, but not her. Was Belle Tyree so much smarter than Katie Hanrahan? Being a college student, could be she was.

But I *know* Paddy better, Katie argued silently. I could press him to work on his book better than Belle. If I'd been working with him all this time, I'd wager he'd be near done with it by now. And if he was, his spirits would be that much cheerier. He wouldn't be looking for all the world like his best friend had died. . . .

The minute she thought it, she was sorry. And glad she hadn't spoken the words aloud.

Because Paddy's best friend *had* died. His older brother.

Could that be what was keeping him from doing the writing? Being heartsick with the loss of Brian? But if that was it, why did he never say so? He never talked about it. Wouldn't that be best, to relieve himself of it, say what he was feeling, even it was a hurting thing to do?

"Come and hear me sing tonight," she said impulsively. He'd come only once before, to a dinner party at an elegant home on Riverside Drive. But he'd left early, during intermission, saying he had had an "idea" and needed to get it down on paper before it slipped his mind. "Anyways," he'd said, "with all these other fine people fawnin' all over you, I'd just be in the way."

That had been the first sign that Paddy wasn't exactly shouting hoorah over Katie's blossoming career.

But if he came to Larchmont tonight, maybe he'd stay longer and they could talk. It would be quiet out there, and peaceful and pretty. Might even put him in the mood to think about taking a trip back home, with all that green surrounding him. "We'll have a good time," she added. "Say you'll come."

This time, he was the one to stop walking, jerking her to a standstill by his abrupt stop. His eyes were very dark as he looked down at her. "If you're thinkin' that hearin' you sing will make me feel better, then you don't understand *anything*."

That was cruel. Why was he being so rude? Stung, she retorted, "It makes *John* feel better. He's said so many times, which is more than *you* said when you came to hear me that time. You never even said you took pleasure in it. And you've not troubled yourself to come to another performance since, even though I telephone you every time and tell you where it is and what time. John comes to all of them, and after he's worked all week, too." She regretted that last part immediately, but he'd made her so angry. How could he be so certain her singing wouldn't help? It helped lots of people forget their worries. They said so, when they came up to her after.

Paddy flushed scarlet. "Meanin', I suppose, that I don't work at all, right, Katie? Well, here's the thing, then. Makes more sense for you to invite John tonight, don't it?" The flush faded and when he spoke again it was without anger. "Anyways, I can't tonight. I have a meeting of me own to get to. Edmund has a British publisher showin' an interest in the book. I'm meeting with both of them tonight. Sorry. I'll come another time, I promise."

But he wouldn't. And even without a meeting to go to, he wouldn't have come tonight, neither, Katie was sure of that. Still, she was willing to let herself pretend he might have if he didn't have to go see a British publisher.

Saying it was later than he'd thought, he put her in a taxicab and handed the driver a wad of bills to pay her fare back to Brooklyn. Katie was bitterly disappointed. If he'd accompanied her home, they could have talked a bit more on the way, and she might have learned what it was that was troubling him so. Or maybe not. She was learning that she had to be very cautious about how she said things, about what she said, never knowing what might set him off. Being cautious about what she said and how she said it did not come easily to her. Hadn't she just proved that?

His kiss when he leaned in through the open window was sweet and tender, but Katie didn't feel his heart was in it. She didn't know *where* his heart might be these days, but she had a feeling it wasn't with *her*.

As the taxicab pulled out into traffic, she turned on the back seat to wave to Paddy one last time.

He was already gone.

# Chapter 13

At the last minute, Katie's singing engagement in Larchmont was cancelled. She was brushing her hair in her room when Lottie called up the stairs, "Flo just telephoned. The people what was havin' the party had to cancel. Some relative died. She said you can do as you please tonight and she'll talk to you tomorrow. I made sure she knew we had Mass in the morning, so she wouldn't telephone then. She said she'd wait until after Sunday dinner."

When Katie had changed out of the new blue dress and pinned up her hair, she went downstairs, intent on calling Paddy. If he'd already had his meeting with Edmund and the British publisher, maybe he'd take her to their favorite place: Coney Island. They hadn't been there since spring, and the weather was perfect now for such an outing. An evening breeze would surely arise to cool off the afternoon heat, and there was no hint of rain. She was missing him something fierce, they hadn't parted on such grand terms, and they always had such fun at the wondrous amusement park.

He wasn't home. Katie let the telephone ring far longer than was sensible, unwilling to give up her thought of a lovely evening with Paddy.

When she finally, despondently, replaced the receiver, Lottie was standing nearby with a suggestion. "You ain't had a Satiddy night off in a while," she said. "Malachy and me was thinkin', why don't we all go to Coney Island? Mary and Tom and their wee one could come, too, if they've a mind to."

John Donnelly, reading the newspaper in the front parlor, overheard. He came out into the hall to say politely, "I wouldn't mind going along, if no one objects. I've heard a lot about the place, but haven't been just yet. I wasn't keen on going alone."

Katie hadn't the heart to say he wasn't welcome. And with a clear eye on matchmaking now that she'd given up on Paddy, Lottie said hastily, "Oh, that'd be grand, John! Won't that be grand, Katie? All of us goin' together?"

Katie nodded and managed a smile for John. 'Twasn't his fault that her and Paddy was having troubles. "It'll be fun," she said, trying to believe it herself. "I'll just run across the street and invite Mary and Tom. I hope Mary isn't feelin' poorly."

Mary was feeling "top-drawer," and an hour later, all seven of them, Bridget perched on Katie's lap, were crammed into Tom's old black car, on their way to Coney Island.

As much as Katie loved the amusement park, it was not at all the same without Paddy. 'Twas Paddy who had talked her into riding the Red Devil Rider, which had taken her breath away; Paddy who had insisted she, too, try to win a prize at various game booths instead of standing by like other girls while the fellow did all the work. He had seemed as thrilled as she when she won a small stuffed panda for aiming carefully enough to knock down three small white ducks in a row in a shooting gallery. He had kissed her on the carousel, unmindful of disapproving eyes.

John steered away from the Red Devil Rider, and any other ride that looked the least bit threatening. He claimed they didn't look "structurally sound" and made it sound like he knew about such things. He said cotton candy was bad for their teeth and that the popcorn-making machine didn't look "sanitary." He did ride the Ferris wheel and the carousel with her, but made no move to kiss her, which was a relief to Katie. John complained about the dust and the noise and the crowd, almost all in the same breath, and more than once.

"You don't like the park, then?" Katie asked irritably as they strolled along the midway. "We don't have nothin' like this in all of Ireland, John. Don't you find it excitin'?"

"Well, sure I do, Katie." But she thought he only said that so she wouldn't disapprove. John did that sometimes, said things certain to get her approval. "It's just . . . say, isn't that your friend Paddy over there?"

Katie's heart skipped a beat. Paddy, here? That couldn't be. He had a meeting.

"Over there . . . on that bench, see? With the girl in the purple dress." Was there a note of smugness in John's voice, or was she imagining it?

She had to turn and look. And there he was. Wouldn't she know him anywhere in the world? He was indeed sitting on a bench, half-turned away from Katie. But she could see enough of the profile she knew so well to be very certain of what she was seeing. And the "girl in the purple dress," she realized, was Belle Tyree. Edmund wasn't with them, nor was anyone who looked like a British publisher. They had the bench all to themselves.

What were Belle and Paddy doing together here in this park that Katie had come to think of as her and Paddy's special place?

He had told her he couldn't come to hear her sing because he had a meeting. And then he had brought Belle *here*.

She hated him. She did. And Belle, too.

"Wouldn't you be wanting to go over and say hello?" John asked.

The suggestion horrified her. Let Paddy see the look on her face? Let him hear the sound of her heart breaking? She would rather jump off the Brooklyn Pier, though she couldn't swim a stroke. "He's busy . . . they're talkin'. About his writin', most likely. We'd best not disturb them. Anyways, we need to be catchin' up with Malachy and Lottie or they'll be leavin' without us." Grabbing John's hand, she tugged him along the midway, never once glancing back in Paddy's direction.

While everyone else in the car sang the praises of the wondrous park during the ride home, Katie fumed. Paddy could have told her the plain truth. Could he not have said, "I'm not comin' to hear you sing because the truth of it is, I'm seein' Belle tonight. What's more, I'm takin' her to our special place."

She knew now why she'd seen so little of Paddy lately. And why he'd been in the doldrums. Probably worrying about how he was going to break the news to her, how he'd tell her that Belle Tyree held his heart now.

Probably scared she'd go into a tizzy over it.

Not *me*, she told herself grimly, ignoring the fact that tears were wetting her cheeks. She didn't even bother to wipe them away. In the car's dark interior, no one could see. It'd take more than a broken heart to throw me into a tizzy. Maybe a while ago, but not now. Not after what she'd gone through on the *Titanic*. And she had her singing, that'd keep her too busy to think about Paddy off somewheres with Belle, and she had Malachy and Lottie and Mary and Tom and Bridget. She had John, too, if she wanted him. What did she need Paddy for? *He* didn't need *her*. He had Belle.

He hadn't changed, after all. Still breaking hearts the same as back in County Cork.

'Twas her own fault. Hadn't she known better? When Paddy kissed her on the *Titanic*, she'd already known both brothers long enough to be aware of Paddy's reputation as a ladies' man. 'Twasn't Brian who was considered the faithless brother. But she had ignored what her head was telling her on board the ship and listened only to her heart. All of her firm resolve not to fall prey to Paddy's charms had dissolved under the sweetness of his kiss.

Paddy had apologized for the kiss, convinced that Katie was Brian's love. She had convinced him otherwise, though it had taken some doing. Paddy was a heart breaker, but he did have a code of ethics. Encroaching on his brother's "territory" went against that code.

I made him see, finally, that is was *him* who held my heart in his hands, Katie thought bitterly, staring out the car window into the dark night, and now look what he's gone and done with it. Stomped all over it with those muddy boots of his!

Still, she couldn't blame him. Belle was pretty, and getting a college education, and her uncle was a successful publisher. Belle could be a great help to Paddy.

And anyways, 'twasn't Belle's fault Kathleen Hanrahan was a fool for a handsome Irish lad with dark, merry eyes and a smile that would melt steel. Should have steered way clear of him and wasn't *that* the truth? Just like the *Titanic* should have steered around that iceberg.

Paddy and Belle. Hadn't she suspected for a while now? She'd seen so little of him lately. 'Course that was partly because she'd been so busy singing. Was that part of the problem, maybe, that she'd been doing so well, and him making no more progress on his book than a mule in mud?

But . . . Katie choked back a cry . . . what earthly good would a singing career be without Paddy? What good would *anything* be?

Katie wiped her eyes. If Patrick Kelleher was too blind to see that no one would ever love him as much as Katie Hanrahan did, if he was willing to toss that away like a sweet potato wrapper, *let* him! She wasn't going to run after him like those silly girls in County Cork. He could just go fly a kite in Central Park! And he could take Belle Tyree with him for all Katie cared.

"John," Katie said in a perfectly normal voice, "would you be interested in goin' with me to the movies tomorrow afternoon?"

Writing a letter to Vassar College declining her admission and scholarship was one of the hardest things Elizabeth had ever done. "I regret . . ." Regret seemed like too small a word for what she was feeling. The word for what she was feeling should have many letters in it, perhaps the entire alphabet. Six letters weren't nearly enough.

But when, unable to give up the last shred of hope, she had mentioned the word "nurse" to her mother, Nola had become so agitated at the thought of being cared for by a stranger, Elizabeth had been forced to hastily reassure her. "I'm here, Mother, I'm here, I'll take care of you," she had to say repeatedly, until her mother finally calmed down.

Nola came home on a bright, sunny Thursday afternoon. Elizabeth left her in Esther's capable hands just long enough to walk to the corner and post her letter. Two young women passed her on bicycles, laughing lightheartedly. Perhaps, Elizabeth thought disconsolately as she walked slowly back to the house, they were on their way to register for college classes, or to sign up for flying lessons, or to take part in a suffrage march beginning in Washington Square. Or perhaps they were on their way to meet two young men in the Village for coffee, where the four would engage in a lively, spirited discussion about workers' rights and unionization, about politics and socialism, about art and books, as Max and his friends did. And as her mother and friends did not.

The fall and winter seasons stretched ahead of Elizabeth like an endless cold, dark tunnel. If it weren't for Max, she would crawl into bed and stay there until next summer. Perhaps her mother would be better by next summer. Perhaps there was still hope. . . .

I can't bear it, she thought as she re-entered the house. I shall not be able to bear it.

Two days later Nola was up and about, fully dressed, taking charge of the household just as she always had. Elizabeth allowed herself to hope again, just a little. Her mother seemed the very picture of health. Impossible to believe she was ill . . . except that Elizabeth had seen her on her knees on the garden path, her face as white as the stone on which she was kneeling. And had sat beside her in the ambulance, Nola's lips bluish, her eyes closed. Had heard the doctor say, "Heart trouble . . ."

"Are you going to sign up for a class or two at CCNY?" Max asked. Though he was working feverishly on his new paintings, he had taken some time off, sensing how unhappy Elizabeth must be. He had asked if she'd like to go for a drive, but she didn't want to leave the house, so they settled on a bench in the rear garden instead. "Anne's taking a couple of classes." Max laughed. "She can never decide which courses to take, so every semester she tosses a toothpick up in the air and wherever it lands on the course calendar, that's the class she takes."

"This is where my mother collapsed," Elizabeth said slowly. It was very hot out. Elizabeth liked the feel of the sun on her skin. Sometimes, when it was really hot, it almost seemed to reach down into her cold, bones. But never quite. "Right over there, that's where she went down. I thought she was dying." Her mother's rosebushes needed pruning again, and Elizabeth thought she saw blackspot on some of the leaves. "I must get someone to see to the roses. Mother will be upset if they're not cared for, and she shouldn't be doing it herself."

"She looks fine to me," Max said, shrugging. "It's hard to believe she has anything wrong with her."

"Well, she *does*," Elizabeth replied testily, moving slightly away from him. "If you'd seen her that day. . . ."

"I know, I believe you, Elizabeth," he interrupted. "I'm just saying she looks really well. Anyway, what about CCNY?"

"I don't know yet. I'll have to think about it. It seems too soon to be leaving her alone. She just got home from the hospital, Max."

"She wouldn't be alone. She has the staff. Or you could ask one of her friends to come over and sit with her, if you think she needs that. Just while you're at class. Did the doctor *say* you couldn't leave her alone?"

He hadn't. Not in so many words. But Elizabeth *felt* as if he had.

Talking about this with Max was a mistake. He just didn't understand. He still *had* two healthy, active parents, even if he seldom saw them.

But he had interrupted his painting to come and see her. On an impulse, Elizabeth jumped up and went to pick a rose for him. One of the yellow ones, by far the prettiest, though her mother's favorites were the pinks. With no pruning shears handy, she broke the stem off by hand, in the process driving a thorn into the fleshy part of her palm. When she cried out, Max was at her side instantly. "I wanted this for you," Elizabeth said, extending the rose with its broken stem. "For coming to see me. You didn't have to. I know you're busy." Tears filled her eyes, not entirely from the pain in her hand. "I wish you could take me back to the Village with you, that's what I wish."

"I wish it too, Elizabeth." He pulled a white handkerchief from his jacket pocket and wrapped it around the injured palm. Then he took the rose from her, slipping it into a buttonhole in his lapel. "Thank you for the rose. I'm sorry you hurt your hand. I'm sorry you hurt in other ways, too, Elizabeth. I wish I could help." He put an arm around her and she leaned into him, laying her head on his chest. She was so tired. She didn't understand that. She hadn't done anything to *make* herself tired. Hadn't been bicycling, hadn't joined a march through Manhattan, hadn't danced the turkey trot all night long at the Victoria. But she *was* very, very tired.

When Max lifted her chin and bent his own head to kiss her, even though it had been a while since they'd been alone, even though Elizabeth missed his kisses and his arms around her, even though she loved him so very much, she felt almost nothing. It was as if mailing that last letter to Vassar sealing her fate and stealing her future had numbed her from head to toe. She almost wept then, with Max's lips still on hers, because she wanted so much to feel what she had always felt when he kissed her. That wonderful, warm, loving and being loved feeling that had so delighted her. When Max was kissing her, when he was holding her, she was never cold. It was the *only* time she was never cold.

She was cold now. In spite of the heat, in spite of Max's loving, passionate kiss, she was freezing.

Perhaps that was why she was so numb.

"What's the matter?" he asked, lifting his head.

The very thought of attempting to answer the question exhausted Elizabeth. Everything, she would have to say, everything is the matter. But Max hadn't come to visit only to hear her complain. "Nothing," she said as brightly as she could manage, "nothing's the matter." She meant, then, to return his kiss, but Nola came out to see to her roses, and the moment passed.

When Max left, he didn't attempt to kiss Elizabeth again. Perhaps, she thought without emotion as she stood on the front steps watching him drive away, he was afraid he'd get frostbite.

It's just as well, she told herself as she went back inside to see if Nola might like to be read to for a while from *The Harvester*. I can never marry Max now. He might as well find some other girl who is free to make him a good wife. I should tell him to do so. It's the fair thing. He's too nice to break it off himself, even though he might want to. It's up to me to set him free. I mustn't put it off. I should telephone him tonight. He'll argue, I know he will, but I shall be very firm. Perhaps I might even tell him I don't love him anymore, that would be the kindest thing to do. I would need to sound as if I meant it. Could I do that?

For Max's sake, perhaps she could.

She tried. That same night, she telephoned him from the drawing room after Nola had gone to bed, afraid that if she waited, she'd lose her nerve. She thought she did quite a convincing job of it, saying she was going to be much too busy to see him for a while, that she did think she might take some classes at the city college, and what with that and taking care of Nola, the smartest thing would be for him to find someone else to keep him company. She would, she said firmly, certainly understand. It just made sense, she said without a quaver in her voice.

But she did not, could not, go so far as to say she no longer loved him.

Then Max's voice, the voice that warmed her to her core, said, sounding amused, "You're not very good at this, you know. You should be grateful you're not yearning for an acting career. No one would ever hire you because you're a terrible actress, and you'd starve." Then his voice deepened further. "Listen to me, Elizabeth. I love you. You love me. I can be patient. I know I'm not always, but for you, for us, I can be. It'll work out somehow. We'll make it work out. We've been through worse than this, remember?"

She remembered.

"So forget about palming me off on some other poor, unsuspecting girl. It's you or no one. Do you understand that?"

"But . . ."

"*Do* you under*stand* that?"

"Yes, Max."

"I love you, you love me. Cozy, vine-covered cottage, someday living happily ever after, right?"

"Yes, Max."

"Good night, Elizabeth."

"Good night, Max."

She wasn't nearly as cold when she went to bed that night as she had been during the hottest part of the afternoon.

But that night there was the dream. Of ice. Of cold water, of screams.

# Chapter 14

Katie gave her aunt Lottie strict orders: If Paddy Kelleher was to telephone and ask for her, she wasn't at home. No ifs, ands, or buts.

"Lyin's a sin," Lottie protested. "What'll I be tellin' Father Doyle in confession on Satiddy?"

"Tell him I made you do it. He knows me. He'll believe you."

It was a knife in Katie's heart, not seeing Paddy, not talking to him, thinking of him with Belle. But she wasn't about to swallow her pride. Mary said, "Why don't you telephone him and ask him to explain it all, then? You're hangin' him without givin' him a trial. That ain't fair."

"It wasn't fair, him takin' Belle to our special place."

On Sunday, she deeply regretted her invitation to John to go to the movies. But he was so excited about it, she would have felt lower than the bottom porch step, backing out. And if she left the house, Lottie wouldn't be lyin' when she told Paddy, if he called, that Katie wasn't home. 'Twould be the truth. No sin there.

The movie, with the strange title of *Quo Vadis* seemed long to Katie, although she did enjoy the exciting chariot race. John seemed to like the film. After the movie, they bought ice cream and ate it during the walk home, which Katie enjoyed more than the movie because they talked only of Ireland.

"I'll take you there, Katie, if you want," John offered when they reached the steps of their roominghouse. "I know how you feel about getting on board a ship. But maybe it would be easier if someone was with you."

It was so sweet of him. He really was kind and thoughtful. In some ways, he reminded her of Brian. Not near as good-looking, but easy to be with. And he'd be faithful as the day was long, too, Katie was certain of that.

"We'll see," was all she would say.

Paddy called, and Lottie said, "It ain't right, tellin' him fibs. Why can't you just talk to him?"

Katie couldn't.

And then he stopped calling.

She cried herself to sleep more nights than she could count. Just as many times, she went to the telephone in the hall and picked up the receiver. But her pride, still intact, took the phone away from her and put it back before she could make the call. When she wasn't with Bridget or talking with John, Flo kept her so busy she had little time to think about her broken heart. And it *was* broken, just as she had always known it would be if Paddy left her.

But her *pride* was intact.

Over the next few months, it became easier and easier to sit with John on a Sunday afternoon, talking, or walk with him to a movie or lend him a book from the library that she'd read and liked. When the weather turned cold and winter arrived in Brooklyn, they sat inside, in the front parlor. They talked of things other than Ireland . . . music, books, movies. Eventually, they went nearly every Saturday afternoon, and when it got too cold for ice cream, they stopped at a nearby delicatessen for coffee and blintzes.

By Thanksgiving, which Katie had spent the year before in Edmund Tyree's luxurious Fifth Avenue home with the Tyrees and Paddy, everyone in her Brooklyn neighborhood believed that she and John Donnelly were courting. Katie herself thought of John only as a very good friend who shared her desire to return to Ireland.

But she made no effort to explain that to anyone.

Not even John.

Her heart slowly began to heal, though it still ached. And her pride was doing quite nicely, what with Flo keeping her booked solid through the upcoming holidays. It made her feel good, all the praise she was getting, and it was comforting to know she hadn't been fooling herself when she'd set out to have a singing career.

On bad days, when she couldn't get Paddy out of her mind, she told herself that if he'd really loved her, he'd have jumped into a taxicab and come to see her in Brooklyn. He knew where she lived. He knew how to get there from Manhattan. If he'd cared that she wouldn't talk to him on the telephone, he'd have done something about it. And he hadn't. So how much could he have cared?

Such thinking usually worked, and Katie went on about her business until the next bad day when she had to go through the same thought process again.

Eventually, the bad days came less often. Soon they would disappear entirely. Until then, all she had to do was keep herself busy with Bridget and John and her singing. Easy as pie.

But she couldn't help wondering if Paddy was making any progress with his book.

He wasn't.

Paddy believed that he knew why Katie

wouldn't take his telephone calls, why she didn't want to see him. It was, he was certain, because he'd not been attentive lately. Even when he was with her, which wasn't often, he was fidgety and out of sorts. And that was because he was getting nowhere with his book. Had barely started it, in fact. Anyways, Katie was doing so well on her own, what did she need with him? Bri would have finished the book by now and been the toast of New York. Maybe that was what Katie was thinking, that Bri would have done better in America than his younger brother. Maybe she didn't want to talk to him on the telephone because she feared she would say that aloud. She wasn't mean-spirited enough to want to do that, but it might slip out.

Still, every day he had to fight the urge to hail a taxicab and travel to Brooklyn to face her. He could talk her into coming back to him. He knew that much. He'd promise to finish the book, even ask her to help him, as she had in the past. She'd seemed to like doing that. He could get her back, was he to try.

But he couldn't do it. He wasn't what she needed. She needed someone steadier, more reliable, someone with a promising future. She had thought *he* had a promising future, after the magazine article sold. He'd thought so, too. Now they both knew better. Edmund was still holding out hope, still encouraging, as was Belle.

But they'd give up, too, soon enough, just as Katie had.

He'd never told her how desperate he was, how impossible it had become to write so much as one sentence about that last night on the *Titanic*. He couldn't let himself relive it. Near frantic, he had gone to Belle instead, explained how he wasn't having any luck writing the book. "If you'll take me to Coney Island tonight," she'd said, "I'll help you with the book all day tomorrow. I love it there, and I hardly ever get to go. I'll bring David, the young man I've been seeing. Telephone Katie, see if she'll come with us." He'd explained that Katie had a singing engagement that night, and when Belle asked why he wasn't going, he'd said, "She don't need me there." He didn't tell her he'd made up a fictitious meeting to avoid watching Katie being fawned over by so many people. Belle wouldn't approve. She didn't hold with lying.

They had gone to Coney Island, which Paddy fretted about some, knowing it was Katie's favorite place. She'd be wounded if she knew he'd gone with Belle. Or mad. But he needed Belle's help. They'd sat on a bench while he explained how the words just wouldn't come. Belle's beau, David, had gone off to get them something to eat and drink and also, Paddy thought, to give them privacy.

It was a waste of time, though. Belle was too

excited to be at the park to concentrate on Paddy's problems. But she had kept her promise about Sunday. That, too, was a waste of time. She had tried her best to help him make a good start on the book. Nothing she said did any good. When she'd gone, and he sat at the wooden table beside the window in his small apartment, pencil in hand, the hand refused to move, the head refused to think, the words refused to come.

It was hopeless.

That evening, when he telephoned the house in Brooklyn, Lottie said, "Katie ain't here. She had some fancy shindig to go to." He'd phoned every night that week. The message was always the same. But he knew Katie didn't have singing engagements every night of the week. And the last time he'd called, he distinctly heard Katie's voice in the background, talking to someone. Most likely that boarder, John, the bank clerk. A fine, sensible lad.

Paddy knew then that Katie wasn't wanting to talk to him.

'Twas a cruel way to end things between them. So sudden like that, with no explaining. That wasn't like the old Katie at all. But he couldn't speak for the new, successful Kathleen Hanrahan. Still, hadn't he done the same thing himself, more than once, back in County Cork? Ended a flirtation without saying why or good-bye? And not felt a shred of remorse over some girl's broken heart?

She didn't want to talk to him. That much was clear as the water in the Shannon. And though it made him feel like he was falling into a deep, black hole darker than the subway tunnels, he knew he was going to let it lie. He wasn't going to go out to Brooklyn and persuade her to change her mind. He didn't have anything to offer her, and that was the truth.

He didn't telephone the house in Brooklyn again.

As autumn arrived, cooling off the days and nights, Elizabeth began to dread the oncoming winter. So cold . . .

Nola didn't seem to mind. The change of season always appealed to her as it provided an excuse for more shopping. Her stamina amazed Elizabeth as they joined the other ladies moving from store to store, their chauffeurs waiting at the curb to receive the packages and store them in the car. Later, they went for tea at Sherry's, where Elizabeth sat silently, sipping hot chocolate while the women discussed the newest fabrics, the silver fox stole Betsy Winslow had ordered, the holiday parties taking shape. Occasionally someone Elizabeth's age, a friend from school, came in to say hello. But with one or two exceptions, they were all engaged and talked of nothing but their upcoming weddings in June. Elizabeth felt totally removed from them and though she listened politely, she was actually thinking of Max.

She thought about Max often. It was the only thing that kept her going. Throughout the autumn months and into early winter he telephoned every night, and once a week Elizabeth left Nola in Esther's capable hands and went to a movie or a play or concert with Max. Nola disapproved, but she said nothing. "I think she knows," Elizabeth told Max as they walked along Madison Avenue holding hands one evening in early December, "that if it weren't for you, I'd jump out of the attic window. She knows how much I hate this life and how desperately I want to leave. Seeing you helps and she knows that. She's not stupid."

"She seems so healthy," Max commented. "I know it makes you mad when I say this, but I really think you should get a second opinion, Elizabeth. Perhaps Dr. Cooper was wrong. Doctors do make mistakes. They're not infallible."

"I did suggest that. A month or so ago. She's determined to have a holiday party. I said it would be too much for her, and she argued that she was feeling fine. So I said, maybe she didn't have anything wrong with her heart after all and why didn't we consult another cardiologist. Well, you'd have thought I'd suggested skinny-dipping in the Hudson. She threw such a fit! Defending Dr. Cooper, accusing me of accusing him of lying, and on and on. Esther came rushing in with smelling salts, worried that Mother was going to have another attack. It was awful. I doubt that I'll be bringing it up again in the near future."

Max had no response to that. They had reached the front steps of Elizabeth's house. "Listen," he said, putting his hands on her arms as she turned to tell him good night, "I'm having a party, too. I think I'll be ready for the unveiling of my new work soon, and I thought I'd make a celebration of it. The night before Christmas Eve. I'm inviting everyone who's been nagging me about showing my work. Say you'll come. I suppose you'll have to fib to your mother about where you're going. Maybe she'll be invited out that evening by friends."

"The night before Christmas Eve? Oh, Max, you didn't pick *that* night! Nola's not going to be out that evening. She's going to be right here. So am I. That's the night of *her* party. She's already sent out the invitations. Can't you have it some other night?"

Max drew away from her, just a bit. "I'm going to have to scramble as it is to finish by then.

Can't do it any sooner. In fact, I probably won't be seeing you until then, because it's going to take every spare moment."

Elizabeth was disappointed, but she knew that as the holidays grew closer, the shopping trips as well as the evening engagements would increase. Getting out of the house to spend time with Max would become impossible.

"Your mother doesn't need *you* at her party, does she? She's got Esther, and the staff. This might be good, Elizabeth, now that I think about it. The house will be so full of people, she won't even notice that you're gone."

Elizabeth mulled that over. Maybe he was right. She would help Nola prepare for the party, right up until the last minute, then she'd slip out as soon as the festivities were well under way. With the house full of people, Nola wouldn't miss a daughter, would she? As long as that daughter returned before the guests left.

But . . . "It would never work." Elizabeth sagged against the stone wall lining the steps. "I just remembered, my mother makes a toast at the holiday party, about halfway through the evening. To the new year. Then my father made one. With him gone, she'll expect me to do it. She'll be looking for me. She'll get upset when she doesn't find me, and if she gets upset . . ."

"You think she'll have another attack." Max

fell silent for a moment, then said heavily, "So does that mean you're not coming to my unveiling?"

Elizabeth hesitated. Max had been the only bright spot in her life during all these boring, dutiful months since Nola's collapse. If it hadn't been for him. . . . "I'll try, Max, I promise I will. I want to be there. Maybe I can slip out right after the toast."

That seemed to be enough for him. His good night kiss was warm and sweet and if Elizabeth stayed in his arms much longer than was proper, it was because she knew that once she went inside, the warmth would leave her. And it wouldn't come back until she was with him again.

# Chapter 15

Preparations for Nola's Christmas party began in earnest. While the menus and shopping fell to Cook, the cleaning and polishing to Esther, Elizabeth's mother took charge of everything else. There were festive holiday gowns to purchase or, if nothing appealing was found in the endless supply of Manhattan shops, to be made. The gowns were most important. Then came decorations, including the tallest, fullest tree, the fattest wreath and garlands, to adorn the Murray Hill house. And there must be entertainment for the guests. Nola had heard of a young Irish girl with a sweet voice. A friend had employed her for his wife's birthday celebration and had recommended her highly. "She sings Irish ballads, none of the vulgar songs coming out of Tin Pan Alley these days. Lovely-looking girl, too. Kathleen something. Her agent is Pauly Chambers, but it's the wife,

Florence, who manages the girl. Common sort of woman, Mrs. Chambers, but not too difficult to deal with. Underpricing the girl, if you ask me." He had given Nola the agent's number. "But call soon. Miss Hanrahan has become quite popular. She'll be booked steadily over the holidays."

Nola had called the following morning and secured Kathleen Hanrahan's services. At a pretty price, she'd thought, but if the girl was popular ... "Nothing good comes cheaply," Martin had been fond of saying. So true.

Elizabeth watched her mother busily preparing for the festivities with a mixture of awe and fear. How efficient Nola was! When the mood struck her. Addressing invitations, making endless telephone calls, conferring with the staff about thousands of details and always, always, finding time to shop. Elizabeth decided that a list of shops Nola had not yet graced with her presence would be very short indeed.

"You're doing too much, Mother," she said after a particularly trying Wednesday in December. They had spent hours traipsing about town in a nasty mix of rain and sleet, shopping for just the right antimacassars for the parlor chairs. If the arms and backs of the parlor chairs, Nola said emphatically, were not covered with the lace doilies during the party, heaven only knew what shape they might be in afterward. The problem was, she was determined to find the lace upholstery covers in "a nice, Christmassy green." Even when there appeared to be none in any color other than white or ecru in all of Manhattan, she continued doggedly searching. Elizabeth finally cried out in exasperation, "Mother, we're wet and we're tired and I'm freezing and what does it *matter* what color they are? Who will care?"

"I will!" But Nola finally gave in, dragging Elizabeth back to the very first store they'd visited to buy an even dozen of the white doilies.

Elizabeth was very annoyed. They could have saved themselves hours of misery . . . oh, what was the use? When they finally arrived home, wet and chilled to the bone, Elizabeth asked, "Mother, does Dr. Cooper know how you're wearing yourself out for this party? I'm sure he wouldn't approve."

Nola patted the last lace doily into place on a white armchair and stood back to admire the effect. "Don't be silly, Elizabeth. I'm not exhausted. I feel better than I have since . . . in a long time. I'm having such fun getting ready for this party."

Elizabeth realized her mother had almost said, "Since your father died" or "since that night." And it *was* true, she did seem more excited than she had in a long while. Happier.

Like a young girl preparing for her first real dance.

Still . . . "You have to be careful, Mother. You mustn't overdo. You really must let the servants take on more. And me. I can do more." What was the point in giving up Vassar, giving up her future, her *life*, if her mother was going to do everything herself?

"Of course you can, darling. Why don't you run along and ask Cook to bring us some lovely hot chocolate? And a few of those gingersnaps she baked this afternoon? That will warm us up. You're shivering again, Elizabeth. In spite of the lovely fire Joseph has made for us."

"Is it any wonder I'm shivering? It's cold outside, and wet, and we were out there for hours." Elizabeth hated being told to "run along." It made her feel like a two-year-old. "We shouldn't have been out in such nasty weather. If you catch cold, Dr. Cooper will blame me. He'll say I'm not taking very good care of you. He'll say we should hire a nurse, who would do a better job of it."

Apparently remembering then exactly why Elizabeth had declined admission to Vassar, Nola did an about-face. She sank into a chair beside the fireplace, put her feet up on the ottoman, and said a bit breathlessly, "You're right, dear. I believe I may have overdone it just a bit today. I wonder if you might fetch me an aspirin or two?"

As Elizabeth left to fetch the aspirin, her mother called after her, "When we've had our little snack, we'll put our heads together and decide what you can do to help me. I'm sure there are many things. I don't know what I'd do without my darling daughter."

How quickly she lost her amazing energy, Elizabeth thought dryly. The minute I said we might need to hire a nurse. Which would, of course, leave me free to do as I pleased. Small wonder Mother suddenly took to a chair.

Too late now, anyway. The first semester was nearly over and it was much too late to apply for the second.

Not that she would leave her mother in the hands of a stranger, even a registered nurse. That was not what her father had had in mind when he said, "Take care of your mother."

Elizabeth sighed heavily as she went into her mother's bedroom and moved to the night-stand. A husband for Nola was still the only answer. But as long as her mother's stand-ards were impossibly high, there was almost no chance of a wedding in the near future. By the time she finds someone who suits her, Elizabeth thought bitterly as she removed two aspirin from the small tin she found in the nightstand drawer, I'll be far too old for college. I'll need a cane just to get around campus.

Nola did enlist Elizabeth's help with the party plans, managing to do this without giving up one ounce of control. Much of the work Elizabeth was assigned came, she decided, under the heading, *Simple idiotic tasks designed to make my daughter feel useful.* Any of the servants could have polished the silver, arranged the flowers, sorted the RSVP's, fluffed the throw pillows, tipped the endless line of delivery men who came in a steady stream to the back door every day during the final week before the party.

Trivial tasks or not, Elizabeth was glad to be busy. It almost kept her from thinking of how the new year held so little promise for her. She didn't *want* to think about that. It would ruin the holidays.

"I should have bought the sapphire blue," Nola said on the night of the party. They still had two hours before the first guests arrived, but she was not one to leave the all-important grooming for the last moments. She was so organized, all that had to be done in the house had been done, leaving only last-minute preparation, which the servants would see to. Now, twirling in front of the full-length mirror in her room, she complained to Elizabeth, "This green makes me look sallow. Why did you let me buy it?"

Elizabeth, reclining on her mother's bed in her robe, her hair wrapped in white cotton rags, laughed. "*Let* you? Mother, if you recall, I did my best to sway you toward the blue. You said green velvet was more in keeping with the season and since you hadn't found the green doilies you wanted, your dress would provide a touch of holiday color."

Nola grimaced into the mirror. "Well, you should have persisted. I look positively sickly."

"You look stunning, and you know it." Elizabeth sat up on the bed. "You *are* feeling well, aren't you?" She was still hoping to slip away after the toast and run off to Max's. But if her mother wasn't well. . . . All of this excitement couldn't be good for her heart.

"I feel fine. It's this *dress* that makes me look ill."

"Mother, you do *not* look ill. Excitement has turned your cheeks quite pink. It's very becoming. In fact, you look amazingly healthy." As Max had pointed out, more than once.

"I *am* amazingly healthy." Nola twirled once more, like a child trying on her first party dress. This time she looked a bit more satisfied with her appearance. "I believe I might even dance tonight, if I can find a partner who is the tiniest bit interesting."

"Dance? Mother, are you sure? Has Dr. Cooper said you might?"

"Darling, I'm not going to hop about the room doing that disgusting turkey trot. So vulgar. But I was thinking, a nice, slow waltz might be lovely."

"You really should check with the doctor first. Is he coming tonight?"

Nola looked shocked. "My physician? Heavens, dear, one doesn't invite one's physician to one's parties."

Elizabeth hated the way her mother used the word "one." It sounded terribly artificial. "Sorry, Mother. I can't think what got into me. Perhaps my sanity has been affected by so many hours of shopping." She got up from the bed to depart for her own room.

Nola was not amused by her daughter's tone of voice. "Wear the white," she ordered before Elizabeth closed the door. "We mustn't clash when we toast our guests, and green goes well with absolutely nothing *but* white."

"I could wear red," Elizabeth teased. "After all, red and green *are* great holiday colors. Everyone would be so impressed with how far we were willing to go to decorate for the holidays." She closed the door on Nola's comment, "I shudder to think how garish that would be."

Laughing softly, Elizabeth went to her room to dress.

She wore the white.

But at the last second, in a small gesture of defiance, she wound a deep-red velvet ribbon around her throat, fastening her grandmother's gold cameo pin in the center. Why should Nola be the only Farr woman boasting holiday color?

If Nola was annoyed by the ribbon, she kept it to herself. Guests were already arriving when Elizabeth came down the wide, circular staircase into the foyer. Nola seemed so relieved to see the white gown, a red ribbon probably seemed inconsequential in comparison to an entire garment of red, which, as anyone with taste knew, only women of ill repute wore.

To Elizabeth, the party was only a stepping-stone to Max's apartment, his unveiling, and his party. She couldn't wait. When her mother's guests told her she looked "lovely," she thanked them and thought, Perhaps Max will agree. As waiters her mother had hired passed her with trays of canapes, she took one and thought, I wonder if Max will be serving food. When the orchestra began playing holiday music, she wondered if Max would persuade Bledsoe to play his guitar, as she'd been told he sometimes did at get-togethers. She'd also been told he played poorly, but at a party, who cared? And when she walked into the ballroom, nearly every square inch of its walls and ceiling draped with garlands, the huge, festooned tree looming over the festivities, she wondered if Max had had time to buy a tree. She had been missing him so . . . hadn't seen him since the night he'd told her about the unveiling, though they had spoken on the telephone every night.

Tonight . . . tonight she would see him. After the toasting was finished, she would slip away from this lavish party and go to a simpler one, the one she really wanted to attend.

But while she was at this one, she intended to keep a close watch on her mother. There would be *no* turkey-trotting in the Farr home, that much was certain. But with a heart condition, perhaps even a waltz could prove dangerous. And her mother had been doing far too much recently.

If only Dr. Cooper had been invited, she could take him aside and ask his advice. He could also be of assistance in keeping Nola calm. She was definitely in a party mood. Stunning in the deep green (which Elizabeth noticed matched almost perfectly the color of the enormous tree at the front of the room, behind the orchestra), she flitted from guest to guest, laughing, making conversation, urging all to eat, drink, and have a marvelous time.

Why, she's actually *flirting*, Elizabeth realized, shocked, as her mother smiled up at a tall, handsome man, who in response, bent to kiss Nola's hand. Elizabeth didn't recognize him, but she decided he had to be European. New Yorkers didn't kiss hands. Which of Nola's many European friends was visiting the city now? Certainly no one would be willing to travel all the way across an ocean to attend a party, not even one of Nola's.

"Your mother looks beautiful," Claire Loomis said as she joined Elizabeth. They had gone to school together. Claire, who had lost no one on the *Titanic*, had made her debut as planned and was now engaged to a banker. She was a sweet girl. Elizabeth had always liked her.

"Yes, she does. But I'm worried about her. She's too ... too excited. She's not well, you know."

Claire looked incredulous. "Your mother? Why, she's the very picture of health. What's wrong with her?"

Elizabeth lowered her voice. "It's her heart. She collapsed last summer. Dr. Cooper says —"

Claire interrupted. "Not Fenton Cooper?"

Surprised at her rudeness, Elizabeth nodded impatiently. "Yes, he said —"

Another interruption. "Oh, Elizabeth, don't you know about Dr. Cooper? I thought everyone did."

"Know what?"

"Dr. Cooper makes a practice of treating only wealthy society people who crave attention and pampering." Claire lowered her eyes in apology, or perhaps embarrassment. But she went on, "He's almost always called in by the patient herself. Then he tells their families that the woman . . . or the man, in some cases . . . has a heart condition. Nothing life-threatening, of course . . . *if* the patient gets plenty of attention and care and is never left alone for too long, never agitated or faced with any unpleasantness." Claire raised her eyes to meet Elizabeth's. "He *did* say your mother has a heart condition?"

Elizabeth could only nod.

"I thought so. That's what he always says." Claire hesitated, then asked, "Is that why you never went off to Vassar? I heard you'd been accepted, even offered a scholarship. But I never heard that you'd actually gone."

Another stupified nod from Elizabeth. Then, rousing herself, she said slowly, "My mother really *does* have a heart problem. She wouldn't lie about something like that." But . . . but there was that letter from Vassar, and then Nola, who had never been truly ill before, had collapsed. Then there was the second letter to Vassar, declining . . . and now Nola was the "picture of health," as Claire had pointed out. "How . . . how do you know about Dr. Cooper? Why didn't I know? Who told you?"

Claire flushed scarlet. "I . . . well, I don't know, Elizabeth, it's just common knowledge.

Everyone knows. He's very popular in our mothers' crowd."

"*I* never heard about him," Elizabeth countered. "That strikes me as odd. As if . . . as if people were keeping the information from me on purpose. Everyone knows he does this, and yet when he began treating my mother, no one *told* me? That seems very odd to me. Unless . . ." Her eyes moved away from Claire to search the crowded ballroom for her mother. When Elizabeth found her, laughing in a small cluster of impeccably dressed and groomed friends, she stayed focused on her. She looked healthier than anyone else in the group. "Unless," Elizabeth finished, "someone made certain I wasn't told about Dr. Cooper."

Claire said nothing.

Keeping her eyes on her vibrant, glowing mother, Elizabeth said distinctly, "I would like you to tell me exactly who first told you about Dr. Cooper. I mean, how you found out about this practice of his of scaring family members into caring devotedly for the demanding mothers and aunts and grandmothers in their lives, and perhaps also the fathers, uncles, and grandfathers." She laughed harshly. "After all, he probably doesn't care what gender the patient is as long as his bill is paid." She tore her gaze away from her mother, fastening it on Claire instead. "*Who* told you about him, Claire?"

Claire's flush deepened. She had no wish to hurt anyone. But Elizabeth was her friend, and wasn't it sad that such a bright, clever girl hadn't gone to Vassar as she might have? And as far as Claire knew, Elizabeth was not even engaged. There was no husband waiting in the wings to care for her. It was really too tragic.

"Your mother." Her voice was a near whisper. But Elizabeth heard her clearly. "It was your mother who told me about Dr. Cooper."

# Chapter 16

Elizabeth stared at Claire. "My mother? When?"

"Last spring. At one of the *Titanic* memorial ceremonies. You were off talking to Max. I was standing with your mother when Marcia Newman walked by. She's Marcia Carter now. You remember, she was engaged to that lawyer, Peter Carter? Her mother disapproved. She thought a lawyer wasn't nearly good enough for Marcia. She had planned to take Marcia back to Europe after her debut, maybe find a title for her to marry. When Marcia insisted she was going to marry Peter, her mother collapsed. Just like your mother. And Fenton Cooper was the doctor who treated Mrs. Newman. He told Marcia he'd discovered that her mother had heart trouble, that she mustn't be upset or get excited about anything. So Marcia broke her engagement, remember?"

Elizabeth did. She'd felt bad for Marcia, knowing how much in love she and Peter were.

"But six weeks later," Claire continued, "Marcia and Peter eloped. I hadn't heard what happened, so when Marcia passed by that day, I asked your mother how Mrs. Newman was. Had she had a second collapse when she heard about the elopement, I asked. Your mother laughed. 'Don't be silly, dear,' she said, 'there is nothing whatever wrong with Dolly Newman's heart. There never was.' Then she laughed and added, 'Dolly knows when to give in gracefully. What else could she do, with her daughter already legally wed? She is now the very picture of health. Of course, she does suffer from indigestion whenever her new son-in-law comes for Sunday dinner.' And she laughed again."

Elizabeth had been stricken speechless. Her mother hadn't really collapsed? She had no heart trouble? "I remember thinking it odd last summer," she told Claire, "that Marcia's mother, rumored to be so seriously ill, had recovered so speedily and so completely. But it had never occurred to me that Dr. Cooper had made a phony diagnosis to keep Marcia from marrying Peter." Elizabeth tried to think clearly. If Dr. Cooper would do that for Dolly Newman, why not for Nola Farr? Not, of course, to keep her daughter from marrying, since that wasn't the problem. To keep her from leaving the city to attend college in Poughkeepsie. To keep her from leaving at *all*.

"Just to make sure I was understanding her," Claire continued, "I asked her straight out. I said, 'Mrs. Farr, are you saying that there are some people in Manhattan who are believed to have heart conditions when they really don't? Because of Fenton Cooper?' And she gave me this look as if she'd just realized she wasn't talking to one of her friends and said, 'Now, Claire, I never said that.' Then she actually tweaked my cheek, can you imagine, as if I were two years old, and said, 'Let's just keep this conversation between us, shall we? At any rate, I believe you completely misunderstood.' Then she left to go find you. But I didn't misunderstand, Elizabeth. And I have to tell you, when we heard that you'd been accepted at Vassar and would be leaving shortly, my mother said, 'Nola will never let her go. Never.' And then we heard about her collapse. I should have put two and two together. I can't think why I didn't." Claire's eyes filled with regret. "I am so sorry that I didn't telephone you and tell you what she'd said to me that day last spring, Elizabeth. Maybe if you'd known, you'd have figured it out. And you'd have gone to Vassar after all."

Elizabeth reached out to pat the girl's shoulder. "No, I wouldn't have, Claire. Don't blame yourself. I would never have believed it. The only reason I believe you now, and I *do*, is, I've been watching her carefully the past couple of weeks, getting ready for this party. Such boundless energy! Not that of a woman with a heart condition, that's for certain. Not once did she seem short of breath, or lightheaded, or weak. Her cheeks were always flushed with color, not the pallor of a patient. Oh, Dr. Cooper came regularly, saying he was here to 'check up on her,' but I suppose that was a plot cooked up between the two of them. I've been watching her tonight, too, flitting around from guest to guest, dancing, rushing to and from the kitchen. She's the healthiest-looking person here. It is so obvious to me now that she isn't sick. I feel like such a fool. Why didn't I suspect she was faking? It's a wonder people aren't coming up to her to congratulate her on her miraculous recovery. How could anyone here think of her as someone who isn't healthy?"

Staring in disbelief at Nola, now waltzing in the arms of the handsome European, laughing up at him, her face suffused with the healthy pink of excitement, Elizabeth had never felt so stupid in her life.

Before she could think how to react to the devastating information Claire had given her, Joseph, doing double-duty as butler for the party, arrived at her side to say, "The entertainer is here, Miss Elizabeth. Name of Kathleen Hanrahan and her agent, the woman Florence Chambers. They're waiting in the foyer. Shall I send them in, or do you wish to greet them yourself?"

Elizabeth needed to escape the ballroom and the sight of her undeniably healthy mother having a wonderful time. "I'll go, Joseph. You can tell my mother they're here."

Walking as if in a daze, Elizabeth left the festivities. Concerned with her friend's pallor and the look of shock on her face, Claire went with her.

"Why, I *know* you," Elizabeth said when she came upon the two women standing just inside the front door gazing around in awe. Elizabeth was addressing Katie, who looked lovely in a simple green gown, her red hair waving loosely about her shoulders. "You . . . you were on the *Titanic*. I remember you. You had those two children with you, and Max put them into a lifeboat. I knew you'd survived. I saw you on the *Carpathia*. You're a singer?"

Katie nodded. Astonished to find herself in the company of the girl from the ship, she couldn't help thinking that her hostess looked poorly. She was as white as the snow just beginning to fall outside, and her eyes seemed shiny, as if she needed to cry but hadn't yet.

There seemed nothing festive or gay about her, yet this was a holiday party, in *her* house. Was she ... Elizabeth, she had introduced herself as ... was Elizabeth not having a good time at her own party? Perhaps she'd had an argument with the handsome, heroic Max and he had refused to come to her party. Thinking of Max made Katie think of Paddy, off somewhere with Belle most likely, and it brought a sharp stab of pain to her heart. Love is so hurtful, she thought as Elizabeth led them to the ballroom, 'tis a wonder anyone ever bothers with it at all. We'd be better off avoiding it the same way we try to steer clear of contagious diseases like the plague and influenza.

As for Elizabeth, she wanted to ask the girl ... Kathleen ... about the other brother, the one she hadn't seen on the *Carpathia*. But she was afraid that inquiring about him would cause the girl pain.

She looks different, Elizabeth thought when she had presented the singer and her agent to Nola, who led them away to discuss the evening's program. She has ... grown up. She's matured from a pretty young girl to a woman, and one who doesn't seem at all aware of how beautiful she is. But there was something else about Miss Hanrahan, something more than just the passage of almost two years' time. Gone was the eager, excited look of anticipation

Elizabeth had seen as the red-haired girl left the tender in Ireland and climbed aboard the great ship. It had been replaced by ... what? Pain? Sadness? Loss? There was something ...

I've seen that look somewhere else, Elizabeth thought as she waited for her mother to return and Claire accepted an invitation to dance. I'm not sure where ... then she realized where. In a mirror every time she looked into one. And in the faces attending all those memorial ceremonies and services for victims of the *Titanic*.

Elizabeth wondered if that look would always be there, no matter how many years had passed since the ship went down.

She was afraid it would.

Still reeling from the revelation of her mother's cruel deception but reluctant to ruin the Irish girl's performance by causing a scene, Elizabeth fought to control her feelings of rage. It was difficult. How dare her mother trick her so cruelly? Cause her such worry, when she was already frightened of losing the only parent she had left? Had Nola never thought of that ... the fear she was instilling in her daughter by her charade? Or had her only selfish thought been to keep Elizabeth by her side, whatever the cost to Elizabeth?

How could such a cruel hoax ever be forgiven?

It was fortunate that the treacherous Dr. Fenton Cooper had not been invited. Fortunate for *his* sake. Elizabeth was so angry and disgusted with his lack of ethics, she thought she might well have seized a carving knife from the buffet table and threatened him with it, forcing him to admit his deceitful practices to all present.

It was so odd . . . she was surrounded by people laughing, dancing, eating, drinking, having a grand, festive time, just as Nola had planned, and yet she, daughter of the hostess, was miserable. *I'm* not having a wonderful time, she thought bitterly.

If only Max were here. He would take her in his arms and listen as she poured out the story of her mother's enormous lie. And then he would say . . .

Yes, Elizabeth? she asked herself. What *would* Max say? You know him so well. What do you *think* he would say?

She knew. She *knew* what Max would say. She could hear that deep, warm voice saying as clearly as if he really were standing next to her, "Finding out the truth about what she's done should set you free, Elizabeth. You know now that she isn't sick. She never was. She lied to you. Your father wouldn't condone that, would he? He seemed an honest person to me. I think he would release you from your promise. I think he would say, 'You owe her nothing now. You are free to go.'"

But Max didn't know how her parents were with each other. It wasn't true that her father wouldn't have forgiven her mother. Martin Farr adored his wife. He'd have forgiven her anything.

But *I* don't have to, Elizabeth told herself. And now that I know she's well, I don't have to stay here. I can leave. I can go to Max's. I can go to his party, have a wonderful time, see his new paintings. . . .

But then what would she do at the end of the evening? She couldn't very well stay at Max's. They weren't even engaged. His friends wouldn't disapprove, certainly not Anne, who was a free-thinker, but even if Elizabeth could somehow manage to throw her own upbringing aside, she was fairly sure Max wouldn't let her. "You'd regret it tomorrow," he would probably say.

Perhaps Anne would take her in, just for a night or two until Elizabeth had figured out a plan. I'll get a job, she resolved, knowing even as she thought it that her choices were limited. I could be a salesgirl at Lord & Taylor, she thought, almost smiling. Who knows their stock better than I? Nola, of course, but she's not looking for a job.

Buoyed by even such an infant of a plan, Elizabeth found a seat on the left side of the ballroom and slid into it just as Nola returned to introduce the evening's entertainment. Judging by the enthusiastic round of applause as the singer entered the ballroom and took her place in front of the orchestra, Elizabeth guessed that many of the guests were already familiar with Miss Hanrahan's talent.

And it *was* talent. Elizabeth listened in rapt attention as the sweet strains of one Irish ballad after another soared out into the ballroom. The girl, so simply dressed in green velvet with no jewelry or ornamentation of any kind, contrasted sharply with the lavishly decorated ballroom. The lush green garlands draped overhead, the round gold and silver globes catching the light of hundreds of candles scattered about the room, the giant tree at the far end, heavily laden with ornaments, all of it suddenly seemed almost gaudy compared to the dignified simplicity of Kathleen Hanrahan.

When the poignant strains of "I'll Take You Home Again, Kathleen" died away, Elizabeth marveled at the sight of tears dampening the faces of sophisticated New Yorkers, including, in at least three cases, men. The singer herself looked nearly shattered as the last note died, her own eyes shining with tears.

"That was truly marvelous," Elizabeth complimented the young woman when she had made her way through the congratulatory crowd. "You have a lovely voice, and your stage presence is impressive. I enjoyed every moment of your performance."

The singer smiled. "Thank you kindly," she said softly. "And I don't mean to pry, but I remember you, too, from the ship, and I was wonderin', is your friend Max doing well? He is a hero to me, you know. I saw him at one of the memorials. Sketchin' away, he was. Is he not here, then? I wouldn't mind thankin' him one more time for savin' the children."

Elizabeth shook her head. "No, I'm sorry. He's hosting his own holiday party tonight. I was invited, but my mother had already planned this party. I wish he could have heard you sing. He's very fond of music."

Happy that the two were still together, Katie asked, "You are both recovered then, from that terrible night?"

Elizabeth had been smiling. The smile vanished. "Oh, well ... I suppose so. I mean, we were so much luckier than others." She stopped herself from adding, It's just that I still have nightmares and I cannot get warm and I lost more than my father that night, I lost my future, too. And Max suffers, too, I think, but won't talk about it. She had a feeling she could tell this girl anything and she would be understood. But not now, not here. Perhaps another time . . .

Katie nodded. "Aye, we were all lucky. But," she added soberly as a beaming Flo appeared at her elbow, "that don't stop the nightmares, does it?"

I knew she would understand, Elizabeth thought, feeling a kinship with the girl. She yearned to sit and talk with her at length. But other people were clamoring to speak with Kathleen Hanrahan, and her agent was urging her to "mingle." "Never know which of these fine folk might be needin' a singer when the holidays is over," Elizabeth heard the woman say.

She did manage to ask quietly just before Miss Hanrahan moved away, "The young men who boarded the ship with you . . . brothers, they looked to be . . . are they . . . did they make it back safely?"

The lovely face clouded. "Only one," she answered, her voice heavy with regret. "Only one. And he . . ." Before she could say any more, Flo Chambers led her away to the guests waiting to heap praise upon her.

So, Elizabeth thought sadly, watching her go, it *was* the older brother they were searching for on the rescue ship. Still Elizabeth knew it was the younger brother the girl loved.

She wondered briefly if the aftermath of that

long, terrible night had been as painful and difficult for Kathleen Hanrahan and the younger brother as it had been for her and Max. Perhaps not. Perhaps Miss Hanrahan had left each and every member of her family miles away in Ireland and thus *had* no deceitful, manipulative mother to contend with here in her new country.

But *I* am not so lucky, Elizabeth reminded herself. And party or no party, guests or no guests, it's time to do something about it.

Taking two deep breaths and letting them out slowly, she went in search of her mother.

# Chapter 17

Though Elizabeth's heart was pounding like the orchestra drums as she sought out her mother, she found it fortunate that most of the guests were gathered around Miss Hanrahan. If the confrontation became an unpleasant scene, perhaps they would be less likely to notice.

Elizabeth wasted no time when she located Nola in the butler's pantry, discussing with Cook the finishing touches on the dessert. Was the chocolate Yule log to have an accompaniment of homemade vanilla ice cream, prepared that very morning, Cook wanted to know, or was the topping to be fresh, heavy cream that had been whipped to a snowy froth?

Typical, Elizabeth thought darkly. Another of the crucial, demanding decisions my mother must make each and every day of her life. These are the matters she uses to exercise her brain.

Well, not *me*. I want much more than that in my life, and I'm going to have it.

"Mother, how *could* you?" she fairly hissed in Nola's face. Elizabeth had waited only until Cook returned to the kitchen, the matter of the Yule log topping decided ... whipped cream, not ice cream ... before planting herself firmly in her mother's path, barring any exit from the pantry. "How could you deceive me like that? As for Fenton Cooper, M.D., he should have his license to practice medicine revoked. Perhaps I shall see to it. Perhaps when I go to Vassar I shall study law instead of literature and one day see to it that the man is drummed out of medicine forever."

Nola grasped the situation immediately. She never flinched, or paled, or flushed with guilt. "We have guests. This will have to wait."

Elizabeth stood her ground. "It can't wait. *I* can't wait. I've waited so long already, haven't I, Mother? Haven't I been the very soul of patience? Every mother in New York should wish for a daughter as patient as I." She had begun speaking quietly, in deference to their guests, though her voice shook. But Nola's insulting lack of guilt or remorse removed every last trace of caution. What did she care what the guests thought? They were *Nola's* friends, not hers ... except for Claire, of course, to whom she would now be indebted for life. Why shouldn't Nola's guests learn of her deception?

Oh, but they already do, you silly girl, a voice in her head scoffed. And Elizabeth realized instantly that of course it was true. Her mother's friends had to know. Hadn't Claire said everyone knew about Fenton Cooper? Everyone except Elizabeth, of course. Nola's friends would have guessed immediately what she was up to. Which explained why they hadn't been half as worried or concerned as her daughter.

She had thought earlier that she couldn't feel any more stupid. She'd been wrong.

"How could you do something so vile?" She was speaking loudly, clearly now, her voice no longer shaking. "You tricked me into believing you were ill! Frightening me, worrying me, how could you? I've lost Father, and you let me believe I might be in danger of losing you, too. How can I ever forgive you for that, Mother?"

Nola did pale then. "I made it very clear to Fenton," she said defensively, "that it was only to be a minor heart condition. Nothing serious. I *explained* that to him. It's not my fault if he disregarded my instructions. I had no desire to frighten you, Elizabeth. I never intended that." Her lower lip thrust forward. "It's cruel of you to suggest that I would be so wicked. I never would."

"Cruel of *me*?" Elizabeth's voice rose another decibel or two. "*I'm* cruel?"

Nola's flush deepened, but her defenses remained strong. "I never knew exactly what Fenton said to you. Remember, I wasn't there. How was I to know he hadn't followed my very precise instructions to the letter?"

"You knew I was *worried* about you. You knew that much. I didn't try to hide it." Elizabeth's tone sharpened. She knew her voice was carrying far beyond the pantry. She didn't care. "Worried enough to turn down my admission to Vassar, and my scholarship. Worried enough to give up any chance at leading my own life, and stay here with you. You knew I had to be *very* worried to give all that up, Mother. And Dr. Cooper *didn't* disobey your instructions. But he also made it very clear that you were not to be agitated or upset. Was that part of your instruction to him? He made it sound as if something very dire might happen if I ignored his opinions. Was *that* part of your instruction? Did you *order* him to give me that impression? Because my leaving for Vassar would have done just that, wouldn't it, Mother? It would have been very agitating and upsetting for you. Wonderful for *me*, mind you . . . but very, very bad for someone with a heart condition who didn't *want* me to leave. Someone selfish and shallow and spoiled."

Nola gasped. "How dare you speak to me in this manner! If your father were here . . ."

"He'd be disgusted with you. Just as I am." But Elizabeth knew it was hopeless. Her mother was never going to admit she'd done wrong. She was never going to apologize or ask for forgiveness. She was too accustomed to doing as she pleased and too unaccustomed to facing the consequences. When there had been consequences in the past, when she'd done something silly or foolish or childish, Martin Farr had "handled" it. He had stepped in and assumed the responsibility for whatever it was, smoothing things over so that Nola's life could go on as easily as it always had.

Elizabeth's anger switched then from her mother to her absent father. You spoiled her so, Father, she shouted soundlessly. You spoiled her, and then you left her to *me*. That was almost as cruel as her deceit. I can't, I *won't*, pamper her as you did, not anymore, not ever again. And if that was what you wanted for her, then you should have climbed into a lifeboat like some other men on the *Titanic*, and stayed *with* her, instead of being so stupidly, foolishly *brave*. You shouldn't have left her. You shouldn't have left *us*.

The force of her fury toward her father shocked and horrified Elizabeth. She *loved* her father. How could she be thinking such terrible things? What was the *matter* with her? It was her mother she was angry with, not her father. Wasn't that why she'd sought out Nola in the first place? Nola had done something so cruel. . . .

But not as cruel as *deserting* both of you, the voice inside Elizabeth's skull muttered.

He had no choice, she argued. She had to clutch the edges of the white wooden shelf beside her to maintain her balance, so shaken was she by her anger toward her father. Captain Smith had *insisted* on women and children only entering the lifeboats. And even if he hadn't, Father knew that was the rule of the sea, and he had accepted that.

Other men got in, the obstinate voice continued. Other men were saved, and to this very day are with their wives, their sons, their daughters. Other men are taking care of their spoiled, pampered wives so their daughters can get married or get a job or march for the vote or go to college, whatever they choose.

Those men were cowards, Elizabeth argued.

Cowards? Yet you just called your father stupid and foolish for being brave.

She hadn't meant it. "I didn't *mean* it!" Elizabeth cried aloud in her pain.

Nola, misunderstanding, nodded. She put a consoling hand on her daughter's arm. "Of course you didn't. You would never speak to me so harshly if you weren't overtired and over-stimulated. We'll talk about it later, dear. I can't imagine what everyone is thinking, what with all this unpleasant shouting going on in here. I'll have to say Cook was being difficult, that's all. They won't believe it, but they'll pretend to, and that's enough for me. Come, let us get back to our guests."

Elizabeth tore her arm from Nola's touch as if she feared contamination. "*Your* guests, Mother, not mine. The only two people my age at this party are the singer and Claire." She added icily, "I have already spent some time with Claire, in case you're at all curious as to how I discovered your cruel deception."

Nola nodded grimly. Elizabeth guessed from the expression on her face that her mother was recalling, too late, her conversation last spring with a friend's young daughter, and deeply regretting how free she'd been with her information about Dr. Fenton Cooper. Still, rather than capitulate, she shifted the blame elsewhere. "I could strangle that girl! When I spoke with her last spring, I wasn't talking about myself. I was talking about other women." Reaching up to pat her hair into place, an unnecessary gesture, Nola added, "That girl talked too much even as a small child. I remember her mother receiving complaints from Claire's school."

"If you knew that," Elizabeth pointed out,

"perhaps you should have chosen someone else to confide in."

"Perhaps I should." Her voice was as calm as the sea on the night of that treacherous iceberg in the North Atlantic. As smooth and shiny as a mirror, that sea had been. But people had died in it, anyway. "Now fix your hair, dear, it's trailing a bit on the left side, just behind your ear."

Elizabeth reached up automatically to recapture the errant strands as instructed. Halfway there, her hand stopped. It will always be like this, she thought. She will tell me what to do, and I'll do it. She'll tell me what to wear, and I'll wear it. She'll tell me where to go and I'll go there. She will give me instructions on what to do, who to see, how to fill my days and nights . . . I won't have to decide any of those things. She'll do that for me . . . as long as I *let* her.

Who is taking care of *whom* here, Father? Elizabeth asked silently.

"You're right, Mother." Elizabeth stood aside to let her mother pass. "Your guests are waiting. You go ahead. I have to do something with my hair." She did *not* add, I'll be right behind you. She would leave the lying to her mother, who was so very good at it.

Elizabeth stood in the pantry doorway, watching as Nola, confident the "family crisis" was over, hurried back to her guests, her party.

Head high, every fair hair perfectly in place, her step youthful, the green gown accentuating her slim figure, she looked like exactly what she was: a beautiful, confident woman who had emerged some nineteen months earlier from a terrible tragedy relatively unchanged. Not unscathed, Elizabeth understood that. Occasionally, she still heard her mother crying in her bedroom late at night. Nola had suffered. But the experience had not *changed* her. Not in any significant way. In spite of that terrifying night in the lifeboat, in spite of her sudden and completely unexpected transition from beloved wife to widow, Nola Langston Farr was still basically the same woman who had boarded the great ship *Titanic* in Southampton on Wednesday, April 10, 1912.

Perhaps that was how she had survived. By *not* changing. Perhaps she believed that by acting as she always had, mimicking as closely as possible the life she'd led before that night, she could pretend the damage hadn't been so devastating, after all. With her husband gone, she could never convince herself it hadn't happened. Even someone as sheltered from reality as Nola couldn't manage that feat. But clinging to every available shred of her *old* life might be the only way she could cling to life itself. Without that, perhaps she would simply have given up. Elizabeth wondered, of the seven hundred and five people who had survived the *Titanic*, how many different ways of dealing with their shock and grief had they found? Seven hundred and five? Probably. Nola's way would only be one of many.

The minute the hem of her mother's dress vanished from sight, Elizabeth was on her way out the front door. She scooped up her purse from the table in the foyer. Without a coat or cape, with no hat to protect her head from the heavily falling snow, without gloves for her hands or boots for her feet, on a cold December night, Elizabeth Farr ran from her house and out into the street to hail a taxicab with no thought for the temperature. She didn't feel the cold.

She was on her way to Max Whittaker's apartment.

# Chapter 18

Max seemed surprised but delighted to see Elizabeth. When he opened the door of his third-floor apartment to find her standing there, he took little notice of how inadequately she was dressed or the snow melting on her hair and dress. Nor did he ask her what she was doing there or how she'd managed it. Instead, he grabbed a hand and pulled her inside, saying excitedly, "I didn't really think you'd come or I would have waited with the unveiling. But I just took the newspapers off a few minutes ago. That's what I was using to cover my work. No one's even said anything yet, they haven't had time, so you haven't missed much. Come on, I'm anxious to see what you think."

The tiny living room was crowded. People were seated on an ugly tweed davenport far too large for the space, and an old wicker rocking chair, which Bledsoe, with Anne sitting on his lap occupied. Other guests were seated or re-clining on the threadbare brown rug, on the windowsills, on the small, wooden kitchen table, and two chairs crammed into a small nook. Elizabeth noticed immediately that the room was ominously silent. There were no voices raised in praise of Max's new work. No one exclaimed in awe or delight. Although all eyes were focused on one or another of a dozen paintings encircling the room, leaning up against the wall, no one said a word.

Max didn't seem to find the silence ominous. "Look who's here everybody!" Max said into the silence. "Elizabeth finally made it!"

Heads swivelled. "Well, hello there, Betsy," Anne said lazily from her spot on Bledsoe's lap, and Norman waved an equally lazy hand. "Mumsy let you out again? My, my, perhaps she's becoming a free-thinker like the rest of us."

Elizabeth didn't answer. No one laughed. And no one took their eyes off the paintings. They all seemed mesmerized.

Max scooped up a pile of sketches from a wooden table beside the couch and motioned to Elizabeth to perch there. Then, standing beside her, an arm around her shoulders, he said, "So? I can't believe I have to beg for opinions from *this* crowd. I expected critiques to be pouring out of you, as they usually are. Go ahead, tell me what you honestly think. I can take it."

No, you can't, was Elizabeth's unspoken response. You don't want to hear what people are thinking, Max, not this time. She felt sick. Because she had noticed the eerie hush the very second she entered the apartment. Her eyes had flown to the paintings displayed around the room. It wasn't hard to guess they were the reason for the lack of gaiety at what was supposed to be a holiday celebration. And what she had seen had sickened her.

They were truly awful. Not in technique. Max was a fine artist. It was the subject matter, and the way it was depicted, that was so horrible. Elizabeth's eyes had darted around the room once, a quick look, then again, a more thorough look. Every painting, without exception, was appalling. An even dozen depictions of . . . her heart began pounding ferociously . . . the sinking of the *Titanic*.

Max was not an abstract artist. That was one of the things she had loved about his Paris street scenes. He painted what he saw exactly the way he saw it, with wonderful attention to detail. These paintings were no different. Artistically speaking, Elizabeth knew they were probably very good. But these were not pictures of the Eiffel Tower or outdoor cafes or gardens in full bloom or lovers strolling along the Seine. These paintings were of a terrible tragedy. Every grim detail of that long, shocking, frightening night stared back at Elizabeth as her eyes moved from one canvas to the next in disbelief. It was as if they were all taunting her, saying, You wanted to forget, but we're not going to let you.

The first group of paintings were of the last moments on board the ship. In the first, Max had caught perfectly the fear in the eyes of passengers waiting on line to climb into a lifeboat. But in a bizarre, haunting contradiction, he had painted in the background people playing cards, smoking cigars, laughing, either unaware of what was happening or in denial.

And while Elizabeth recognized the painting as truth . . . it *had* been like that for some . . . it sickened her. Those people who had been unwilling to accept reality, who had insisted to the end that the ship was not about to sink, that they weren't leaving a "warm, comfortable" ship to go out on the cold, dark sea in one of those "flimsy" lifeboats, those people had all perished. They had waited too long. What she and the rest of the world had later learned was, by the time they had accepted harsh reality and were ready to abandon the sinking ship, there were no lifeboats left. They would not be leaving . . . alive.

Max had captured their terror, too, in the second group of paintings. The faces in these works were more painful to look at than those in the first. These passengers left on board, clinging to the rail as the ship climbed ever higher in the water, nearly perpendicular to the deep, dark water waiting below, knew they were about to die a horrible death. The ocean temperature was below freezing. Even those who were expert swimmers had to know they had no chance of survival in such conditions. And those who had climbed up to cling to the rail at the very highest point of the ship knew that should they lose their grip, the resulting fall would either dash them to pieces when they struck some part of the ship on the way down, or kill them when they hit the water However they died, they knew that death was at hand.

All of this was reflected in the ugly, twisted, faces Max had painted. The mouths were opened in screams, the eyes wide with terror. And in a touch of irony not lost on Elizabeth, Max had painted out on the sea surrounding the ship a trio of lifeboats which were, disgracefully, no more than half filled. This, too, was truth. But it was embittering to gaze upon. Her father could have been in one of those boats, as could many other people who had perished. She tried never to think about that, because it made her so angry. And now Max had painted it, forcing her to think about it, to remember.

The third group of paintings was almost impossible to look at for more than a second. It was, she guessed, from what little she had seen of the area, a depiction of steerage passengers trying in vain to break through the locked iron gate that kept them from the upper decks and safety. There were men, women, and children. Some of the faces expressed terror, others fury, while most of the younger faces were bewildered or frightened.

Elizabeth knew that most of the people in the painting had never made it through that locked gate.

But the last group was the most painful. The backgrounds were all somber tones of purple and brown and black, but the figures, the people, were done in brighter colors: reds, yellows, greens, as if by coloring them so vividly, Max meant to point out how alive they had once been. The scenes were grim. People falling to their death as the pull of gravity tore them from the rail. The ship breaking in two, the detail in this painting so graphic Elizabeth could almost hear the ripping, tearing sounds just as she'd heard them that night from the lifeboat. The worst of the lot were the scenes of the ocean after the *Titanic* had slid beneath the surface, disappearing from view. The now-smooth, flat, dark water was broken in Max's last three paintings by the bodies of floating victims encircling the lifeboats, including one child, lifeless, its eyes closed, improbably clutching a glassy-eyed doll under one arm.

It wasn't like that, Elizabeth cried silently. We weren't that close to the victims, we didn't ignore them in the water, not like that. At least, it hadn't been like that around her lifeboat. If it had, she would never have forgotten it, never. Bad enough that she had heard the screaming. Still did hear it. Probably always would. But she had not seen what Max was depicting here.

He was clearly saying, "More people would have been saved if the survivors in the lifeboats had helped." And that, too, was a truth. She knew that. Everyone knew it.

But only Max had painted it, which was the same as saying it aloud.

"No one's going to buy these, Max," Bledsoe finally said into the shocked silence. "As art work goes, they're technically damn near perfect. The detail, the colors, they're great. But no one's going to buy them."

Other people murmured agreement.

Max frowned. "I didn't paint them to make money. I thought you'd understand that." He glanced at Elizabeth. "*You* do, don't you, Elizabeth?"

She didn't. She had no idea why he'd painted

them, couldn't imagine a reason. There couldn't *be* a reason. When the only response she could give him was a slow, sad shaking of her head, he looked hurt and confused.

Only Anne said, "I like them. They're, well, they're scary, but they're good. I like them."

You would, Elizabeth thought angrily. Anything to be different. But then, Anne, you weren't *there, were* you? You have no idea how these paintings will twist the knife already imbedded in the heart of every survivor, in the heart of every relative of every victim. You don't understand. How could you?

It was then she noticed something in the first painting that she'd missed, and it took her breath away. One of the faces waiting on the lifeboat line was her father's face. There was no question about it. Max had captured his likeness perfectly. The face seemed incredibly sad but brave, the head up, the shoulders back. The eyes were gazing out at sea. She realized then that he was standing alone, that what he was looking at in the distance was a lifeboat already launched, in which sat, among other passengers, a young girl wearing a large red hat and an older woman in a similar hat of royal blue.

Their hats, hers and her mother's, had been black. But Max had used brighter colors, just as he'd done in the other paintings.

Elizabeth began crying quietly. "Oh, Max," she whispered, unable to look up at him.

Obviously reeling from an unexpected reaction to his months of work, Max bent stiffly toward her. "What? What did you say, Elizabeth?"

She didn't answer. She couldn't.

A tall boy named Gregory who had been sitting on the floor stood up and said, "You know what, Whittaker? I lost an uncle on the *Titanic*. I'm all for freedom of expression and all that, but *I* think you've crossed the line here. I thought the postcards and the songs and the souvenirs were bad, but this . . . this is a lot worse. If I were you, I'd burn every single one of these and start over. And pick a different subject next time, all right?" To his girlfriend, also climbing to her feet, he said brusquely, "C'mon, Libby, let's get out of here, before our holiday mood is completely ruined."

"I guess he doesn't like my paintings," Max said with forced lightness when the two had gone. "Well, I didn't expect everyone to like them. And Bledsoe, it doesn't matter if they don't sell. That's not why I painted them."

Elizabeth lifted her head. "Why did you paint them, Max?"

Sensing a confrontation they had no desire to participate in, the other guests got up to leave, mumbling various excuses. Another holiday party . . . a concern about traffic in the falling snow . . . a rally to attend early the next day. One or two said, "Interesting work, Whittaker" or "I can see why you've been so busy lately," but no one, not one person except Anne said they liked Max's new work. And when Bledsoe, sending Elizabeth a sympathetic smile, led Anne from the apartment, she called over her shoulder, "Remember, Max, the important thing is to do as you please!" rather than complimenting him again on the work.

When they had all gone and Bledsoe had closed the door, Max knelt by Elizabeth's side. Looking up into her face, he asked with concern, "You don't like them either? You look upset. They've upset you? The paintings?"

Elizabeth jumped to her feet. "Of *course* they've upset me, Max! They'd upset anyone, even people who weren't *on* the *Titanic*! They're . . . they're horrible! I don't understand . . ." Her eyes caught sight of her father's face again, and she began crying. "You painted my *father*. How do you think it makes me feel to see him standing on deck all alone, my mother and I already gone? Why didn't you just *stab* me, Max? It couldn't have hurt any worse than that painting hurts me."

His face went bone-white, and he took a step backward, away from her. He had put up a puny, scraggly Christmas tree in one corner of the room and decorated it haphazardly with large red colored lights. They were on, and the reflected red playing across his features contrasted sharply with the sudden loss of color. "Elizabeth, I . . ."

"All these months you've been saying how hard you were working, and you never once even hinted that you were painting something like this. You didn't tell me because you knew I couldn't bear it," she accused. "And you're right. I can't. It's cruel, Max, it's so cruel. People are trying to recover, to get on with their lives, to put that terrible night behind them. And then," she waved a hand to include the paintings, "you bring it all back."

His lean, handsome face twisted in pain. "Oh, God," he breathed, "is *that* what you think? That I was trying to bring it all *back*? I wasn't, Elizabeth, that's not what I was doing." Looking ill himself, he sank into the wicker chair, putting his head in his hands.

Elizabeth fought a desperate desire to rush over and put her arms around him. This was Max, whom she loved. There had to be a reason why he had done this. It was cruel, and Max was not cruel. Never cruel. "Then what *were* you trying to do?"

He didn't answer for a few minutes. When he lifted his head, his face looked so tortured, so torn, Elizabeth nearly wept for him. "What, Max?" she persisted quietly. "What were you trying to do?"

"Get rid of it," he said, his voice anguished. He put his head in his hands again. "I was trying to get rid of it. All of it. So I put it on canvas. I didn't know how else to do it."

"Get rid of it?" Hadn't he already done that, months ago? He'd seemed to. And he'd told her to stop thinking about it. As if that were possible.

Maybe it hadn't been possible for him, either. Maybe she'd been wrong. . . .

Max nodded. "Yes. Get *rid* of it." He shook his head, and when he lifted his face to her again, she saw tears in his eyes. "I shouldn't have done it. The minute I saw the look on your face, I knew I'd made a terrible mistake. They are as ugly as that night was, I can see that now. But when I was painting them, I wasn't thinking that way. I was just trying to get it all out, away from *me*. So that I could sleep at night again. So the attacks would stop."

She did move toward him then, sinking to the floor beside his chair to look up at him. "Attacks?"

He described then, in agonizing detail, the nightmares he suffered from, terrible, black dreams of drowning in a deep, dark pit whose walls were as slippery as silk. But worse, he told her, were the episodes when he was fully awake. They came upon him without warning, and they came often. "It's as if I'm suffocating. It's the same way I felt when I was under the water, before my drunken rescuer came along to snatch me up to the surface and drag me to a lifeboat. I can't breathe, any more than I could then. My chest feels like the *Titanic* itself is sitting on top of it. Most often, it happens at dusk, just as the sky begins to darken. I'm not sure why. It wasn't dusk when I was tossed into the ocean. But when it happens, I can't breathe, or swallow, or talk. Sometimes it hits me when I'm painting, or eating, or talking on the telephone. It's as if every last breath of air has been stolen from all around me and my lungs are filled with cotton . . . or, more likely, saltwater. Dark, frigid, saltwater."

Elizabeth reached up to touch his hand. "Max, why didn't you say anything? You never told me."

"It has even happened," he continued, "when I've been with you. I would have to stop talking in the middle of a sentence, trying to get my breath back. You never noticed."

"I'm sorry. You should have said something. I had no idea. You hid it well."

He shrugged, seeming a bit calmer. "You couldn't have helped. I guess that's why I never told anyone, not even you, because I knew it was something I had to handle on my own. When nothing I tried worked, that's when I came up with the idea of the paintings. I figured, other artists paint reality, why not me? I knew I could do it. The pictures were so clear in my head." He shuddered. "Very clear. Anything that I hadn't seen with my own eyes, I just pictured from what I'd heard and read afterward."

Elizabeth thought for a moment, wanting desperately to say the right thing, words that would make Max feel better. "The paintings are very . . . accurate. I don't think photographs could be any clearer than the images you put on canvas. You are very, very talented, Max. They're very good. It's just . . ."

He nodded. "I know. The subject matter. Not fit for human eyes. But people should know. I never meant to hurt *you*. The look on your face. . . ."

"It's all right, Max." She held his hand tightly, fixing her eyes on his. "I know you never meant to hurt me. You wouldn't ever do that, not on purpose." She paused, then asked, "Did it work?" She waved her free hand to encompass the paintings. "Did painting these scenes do what you'd hoped? Are the nightmares gone? Have you had any attacks since you finished the last scene? When *did* you finish?"

"This morning. I put the finishing touches on

the last one this morning. So I don't know if it worked or not, not yet. But . . ." He leaned forward to touch Elizabeth's cheek. "Just telling you helped. That's pretty strange. I never expected that. I thought talking about it would make it worse. I was sure that bringing it out into the open would somehow make it bigger, more real, something . . . give it life, I guess. Not that it didn't already have a life of its own."

"I just wish you'd said something sooner," said Elizabeth. "What's the point of having someone to love if important things aren't shared? I don't expect you to tell me everything, Max. You have a right to your private feelings, just as I do. But we were both suffering. It might have been easier if we'd shared that."

"I couldn't."

"I know. But it still makes me feel bad. Knowing you were going through all that and not being able to help you." Elizabeth smiled. "I was mad because I thought you weren't feeling anything. You kept telling me to forget about that night, put it behind me. And the whole time you were doing *this*." She waved at the paintings again. "I should be really mad at you now, just for making me think you were getting over it and I wasn't. You know that wasn't fair."

"No, it wasn't. And it was stupid. I should have been more honest."

They sat in silence for a while, heads together, Max's arm around Elizabeth. "So, you forgive me?" he asked finally, sitting up straight but maintaining his hold on her hand. "You don't hate me?"

"No, Max, I love you. Just don't keep things from me, all right? Not big things, anyway." Elizabeth paused, then asked, "What are you going to do with these?"

"I don't know yet. I'll have to think about it."

Elizabeth hesitated, then said, "Don't destroy the one of my father. I don't want it just now. I'm not ready. But could you please keep it? Maybe later, when it doesn't hurt so much, I might want it."

"Are you sure?"

"No, I'm not sure. But I think maybe . . . it's a wonderful likeness of him, Max. He looks so . . . brave."

"He was brave. Right up until the very last minute. I'll keep the painting for you, Elizabeth. You just let me know when you're ready to own it, and it's yours."

"Thank you. I'll be careful not to hang it where my mother can see it. I don't think she could stand it. But then," Elizabeth added with a wry smile, "that won't be difficult, since I won't be living in her house."

Then she told Max everything that had happened before she arrived at his apartment.

# Chapter 19

"They seemed like nice enough people," Flo commented on the drive back to Brooklyn after the Farr Christmas party. The snow had ceased to fall, but a slick, light coating of it covered the road, forcing Flo to drive slower than usual. "And a fine house it was. Shame about the father. *Titanic*, it was. Terrible thing."

"I was on that ship," Katie said without meaning to. The words slipped out easily, surprising her. She never talked about it anymore. She had learned not to, from Paddy. And then, although John was a good enough listener, he hadn't been there that night, so what was the point in speaking to him of it?

Flo was so shocked, the car swerved on the road. "Go on, you weren't! On *that* ship! And never mentioned it before?"

"You never brought it up before. And anyways, it's not such a good thing to talk about.

'Twas a terrible night, not somethin' people take any joy in remembering."

"But you survived. One of the lucky ones, sitting right here in my car. That's a wonder."

"Yes, I was lucky. And Paddy, too."

Flo glanced over at her sharply. "I thought it was John you were keeping company with now. Thought you were all over Paddy."

"I am. I was just sayin', he survived, too. His brother didn't. And his body wasn't recovered, like some of them. But Paddy survived."

"That must be a hurt," Flo commented. "Losing his brother in such a way. Wouldn't *that* give you nightmares, though? Thinking of your own brother, down there in the deep, dark sea." She shuddered. "Wouldn't imagine your Paddy ever gets a good night's sleep."

"I wouldn't know. He never said. And he's not my Paddy." It was upsetting . . . how saying that still pained her so. She hadn't seen or talked to Paddy in months. That girl, Elizabeth Farr, had said she had "great stage presence." Maybe that just meant pride was keeping her head up. What she really wanted to do was bury it in a pillow and bawl her eyes out, she still missed Paddy so.

Not that bawling would do any good.

They were still nearly ten blocks away when they saw smoke in the distance. It was thick and dark, spiraling steadily upward to bruise the night sky, turning it a deep, ugly purple.

Noticing the smoke, Katie sat up straight on the seat. "That smoke there, see it? It looks to be near my aunt's house. Maybe you could go a bit faster?"

But other drivers returning from a night out in the city had noticed the smoke, too, and had slowed their pace, sensing excitement and fearful of missing it. Flo had no choice but to proceed cautiously. Katie, anxious for her aunt and uncle's safety, began fidgeting, sitting very far forward on the seat and peering through the windshield.

By the time they had less than three blocks to go, the smoke had intensified, a high wall of gray wool so thick, it was impossible to discern which roominghouse might be the victim. Katie couldn't even be sure on which side of the street a fire might be raging. She knew only that it *was* raging, knew that what she was seeing from a distance was no boiling pot overturned on the stove, no ashes from a coal burner setting a small throw rug ablaze, no heated iron burning a hole the size of a silver dollar into a wooden ironing board. It took more than a small fire to spew forth such giant clouds of evil black smoke.

With two blocks still to cover, Flo's car, held

captive in a long line of curious drivers, was moving at a snail's pace. Katie could stand it no longer. Taking advantage of the lack of speed, she shoved the door open and jumped out. As late as it was, almost eleven o'clock, she could see just fine. There were streetlights, and lights from houses. Besides, she'd walked this avenue many times with John or with Mary and Tom. She knew the way.

Flo shouted after her, "You stay away from that smoke! It'll be the ruin of your voice!"

Katie was already racing up the street, slipping and sliding on the slick sidewalk. Heart pounding, holding up the hem of her green dress to keep from tripping, she ran toward the smoke. She saw no flames, but perhaps she was still too far away. Another block, and now she could see the source was a house on *this* side of the street, not on her aunt's side. Her knees would have gone watery with relief then except that just as quickly she realized that the house directly across the street from her aunt's was Agnes Murphy's. Where Mary and Tom lived. And Bridget.

Katie ran faster.

When she was close enough to realize that it was indeed Agnes Murphy's house spewing smoke, her eyes quickly scanned the scene for some sign of a skinny little girl with bright red hair. There were no small children present. It was late. They were safely in bed, asleep. Most of the neighborhood men worked the night shift at a nearby factory. They wouldn't be working on Christmas Eve, but that was tomorrow night. Not tonight. That left only elderly neighbors, some with nightwear poking out from beneath their winter coats, to gather on the lawn.

Katie saw no sign of Bridget.

But her eyes did locate Mary, sobbing in the arms of her landlady. Tom was away at work, and wouldn't be home until seven in the morning. Katie pushed her way through the crowd. The wind had changed, now blowing the smoke toward the rear of the house. Though there was plenty of the thick, dirty gray stuff pouring from the open front door and first floor windows, she saw no flames. Perhaps there was no real fire, only smoke, though Katie couldn't imagine how that could be so.

She ran to Mary and Agnes. "Where is the baby?" she called, tapping Mary on the shoulder. "Where is Bridget?"

Incapable of speech, her face still hidden in Agnes Murphy's ample bosom, Mary could only point. She pointed straight at the house.

"She's in there?" Katie cried, horrified. "Has no one gone in after her, then?" She whirled, her eyes flying accusingly from one face to another. She saw no one who looked hale and hearty enough to enter a smoke-filled house. They were all too old.

Katie turned back to Mary. "Are you certain sure she's inside?"

Silent nodding from Bridget's mother.

"She was sleepin', Mary was," Mrs. Murphy said over the top of Mary's head. Her tone was not unsympathetic, even though it was her house that might be burning. "Had herself a bad day, so she went to bed early. I was next door, havin' a cuppa tea with Mrs. O'Donnell, when we seen the smoke. Come right over here and woke up Mary, but the smoke was so thick we couldn't stay in there. 'Twas grabbin' us by the throat and yankin' all the breath out of us. When we tried to call for Bridget, we swallowed smoke so bad, nothin' came out. I don't . . ."

But Katie was already gone, pushing open the gate and dashing up the cobblestone path toward the smoke-filled house.

She paid no attention to the warnings shouted after her.

# Chapter 20

Had it not been for the image of Bridget's small, pale face firmly lodged in Katie's mind, she would have turned and fled instantly from the thick clouds of smoke billowing through the open front door. There were no flames, but the smoke itself engulfed her, tearing at her throat. She was coughing even before she stepped over the threshhold.

But Bridget was inside. . . .

As Katie hesitated for a second in the doorway, her hands over her nose and mouth to protect them, she heard the faint wail of a siren. Too distant, much too far away to be of any help quickly. And how, then, would a fire engine make its way through that long line of autos crawling along the avenue hoping to see something exciting? What if the siren she was hearing wasn't even headed her way? Could be going somewheres else, to a different fire, maybe, or to a car wreck because of the slippery roads.

She dared not wait. Bridget couldn't wait.

Katie plunged headlong into the thick wall of dirty gray.

Once inside, she felt as if she had been swallowed up by a giant steel-gray monster. She could see nothing. There was not the tiniest shred of light to help her find her bearings. The smoke was so acrid it sent tears streaming down her cheeks. Her hands left her face to yank her skirt and petticoat up to cover her nose and mouth. This helped only a little. She couldn't be sure exactly where the staircase was. In all that gray wool, there seemed to be no left, no right, no stairs. . . .

She dropped to her hands and knees, thinking to get her bearings by crawling along the floor and using touch to locate various pieces of Mary's furniture . . . the couch along the front wall, the parlor piano, the telephone stand decorated with seashells positioned along the wall just below the stairs . . . if she could find that stand, she could find the stairs. If it was the piano she found first, she would know she had moved in the wrong direction.

She found the seashell stand. She was already coughing so hard, the crawl from doorway to stairs took ten times longer than it should have. And crawling with one hand holding the skirt and petticoat over her mouth was very difficult. But she had no choice. She had intended to call for Bridget as she went, but the first time she opened her mouth to do so, the only sound that emerged was a harsh croak. Smoke rushed in, gagging her, and she shut her mouth quickly, only to have it forced open again by a wracking cough.

The realization that Flo had been right, that the smoke had already damaged her voice, making it impossible to call for Bridget, was frightening. Finding the child would take so much more precious time now that she couldn't summon her by voice. Katie almost turned around then and went back outside. But she had heard no sirens arriving at the house, no sound that help was at hand. She couldn't desert the child. That would be too cruel.

Brian hadn't deserted the steerage passengers on the *Titanic*, even when he knew there was no hope of rescue, knew he would not be saved. Still he had stayed.

I'll stay, too, Katie vowed, until I find Bridget.

She still saw no flames. That was a blessing. Perhaps there was no real fire, perhaps something in the house . . . the old coal stove in the basement, maybe, was spitting out the smoke. Katie had no idea if that was even possible, but the thought was comforting so she clung to it as she slowly, painfully, made her way up the stairs, crawling on her stomach, tears pouring from her red and swollen eyes.

Why, Katie thought in a flash of anger as, exhausted, she reached the top step, had Mary gone outside without her small daughter?

If anything terrible happened to their only child, Tom would never forgive his wife.

A small orange flame, like a curious kitten peeking around a corner to see who was there, darted straight at Katie from the corridor. It shocked her. It wrecked her notion that the house held only smoke. She heard, then, a new sound. Like feet tramping on small, dry twigs, snapping them in two, or on dry autuman leaves. She and Paddy made sounds like that when they walked in Central Park in the fall.

But no one needed to tell her these were not the sounds of feet in the park. This snapping and crackling was the sound of furniture and framed photographs and the pages of books and the soles of shoes and the glass of mirrors being consumed by flames. She pictured the very walls themselves being devoured by the fire, leaving nothing behind of Agnes Murphy's house but smoke and ashes.

Katie didn't care about the house or anything in it. All she cared about was finding Bridget, toting her safely from the house to give her back to her mother.

Her eyes burned so furiously, she had to

keep them closed. It made no difference, since she could see nothing. She was surrounded by a thick, gray wool cape. And it wasn't her eyes that worried her, it was the constant coughing. How long before the thick, cloying smoke pulled every last breath out of her and stopped her heart forever?

Only once in her life had Katie Hanrahan been as frightened. In the belly of the great *Titanic*, wandering panic-stricken along its silent, narrow corridors, desperate to find a way up, to light and air and safety, she had been terrified that she and the two children left in her care would die down there. Paddy had saved her then. But Paddy was far away now, in the city, probably somewhere with Belle, not knowing Katie needed him again.

I was mean to him, she thought dazedly as, gasping and choking, she pulled herself up into the hall. A second shoot of flame reared its nasty head, darting around the corner to tease, I *dare* you, I dare you to keep coming! Katie ignored it, and began sliding along the corridor floor on her stomach. I should have told Paddy why I was being so sour with him, it wasn't fair of me to turn him a cold shoulder without sayin' why. 'Twas cowardly, if nothin' else. If I could just see him again, for a minute. . . .

The agonizing climb up the staircase had left her drained, her chest aflame like the building itself, and there was an ominous roaring sound in her ears. Comin' from my brain, she told herself. It's mad it's not gettin' enough oxygen and it's roarin' in anger.

Dizzy, so dizzy . . . sleep would be just the thing. If she just took a tiny little nap, just the smallest forty winks, maybe when she woke up the nasty old fire would be gone, the smoke cleared. Then she would find Bridget and they would go outside together into the clean, fresh air.

That seemed to Katie's oxygen-deprived brain a fine idea. She might have followed it had she not, as she stretched an arm out over her head in preparation to lay her head on it, encountered with her fingers a small, human hand. The hand was limp, lifeless, but . . .

Gasping in shock, she clutched at the hand. She tried to call out Bridget's name. Impossible. Her vocal cords, seared by heat and smoke, no longer functioned. Flo would be so angry.

Katie's head cleared suddenly. She had found Bridget. She had done half of what she came to do. Now she had to get the other half done. She had to get both of them out of this deathtrap of a house and into fresh air and safety if they were to live.

She had no idea how she was going to do that.

# Chapter 21

Yanking her skirt up over her face again, Katie crawled over to the small figure. She knew to feel the tiny wrist for a pulse. It was faint . . . very faint . . . but it was there. Bridget was still alive. But she needed to be taken from the smoke-filled house.

How? Katie would have shouted aloud if she'd had a voice. *How?* She was so weak herself, she could barely crawl on her own, let alone carry even as small a child as this one.

Why had no one come to help them?

Anger pulled her up onto her hands and knees. I did not survive the worst sea tragedy in history, she told herself grimly, when so many others did not, only to perish in a fire in a Brooklyn roominghouse!

The voice that Katie heard next was not her own. It was her ma's. "Well, if you're goin' to do what you came in here to do," her ma's voice said, "you'd best be about it."

Katie lifted her head. "Ma?"

No answer. Sheila Hanrahan had said all she meant to say. Now it was up to Katie to heed or ignore her mother's advice.

Didn't seem like she'd have heard it in the first place if she was meant to ignore it.

There were no new flames taunting her, and the smoke seemed to have lessened just a bit. Could be her ma had scared it away. Reaching out tentatively with both hands, Katie clasped her hands around Bridget's small wrists. She could still feel a pulse, which seemed a great wonder to her. Bridget's spirit must be very strong, then. That thought renewed her own strength, and holding tightly to the two delicate wrists, Katie began inching her way backward, still on her stomach on the floor. She had no free hand now to keep the green skirt and petticoat over her face. But her head had cleared, as if her mother had somehow filled it with life-giving oxygen.

If she could drag Bridget to the top of the staircase, staying flat to avoid the thickest smoke, they could slide or even tumble down the stairs to safety.

If she could find the stairs.

She couldn't.

She wasn't sure exactly how she'd got

turned around. Perhaps when she'd crawled to Bridget. Though she crawled the length of the corridor, pulling the little girl along with her, she never came upon any stairs. Perhaps they'd collapsed. Or perhaps they were there and she couldn't see them in all the smoke.

This, Katie thought despairingly, must have been what it was like for Brian when he was thrown into the Atlantic Ocean. It would have been as dark and murky down there as it is in this hall. Like me, he wouldn't have been able to see, or get his bearings, or think what to do. The difference was, Brian would have frozen to death almost immediately in that below-freezing water, and so he hadn't been able to save himself. It was not cold in the hall of Agnes Murphy's roominghouse. Katie felt she had no excuse for not saving herself and Bridget. Brian would expect her to, considering how much more fortunate she was than he.

Without a staircase, they would have to leave the house some other way.

Katie slid her body around on the hot floor to kick out behind her, seeking a door, any door, that would allow them to escape the smoke-filled hall. If she could find a room that wasn't being consumed by fire, there would be a window in it. She could open the window and let in blessed fresh air.

The thought spurred her on, and she slid and

kicked out at the wall behind her, slid and kicked, never letting go of Bridget's wrists for a second. She didn't realize she'd come to a door until it burst open after several sharp smacks with Katie's booted foot. Still pulling the unconscious child, she used her knees and feet to propel them both backward. Her left arm was beginning to pain her fiercely, and she realized that it had been burned. She wasn't sure how, hadn't been aware of a flame touching her. But one must have, because she knew a burn when she felt it, and when she turned her head to look, she saw that the sleeve of her green dress was blackened just above the elbow.

Flo wouldn't like that, either.

The room was not as thick with smoke as the hall had been. And when Katie lifted her head and with tremendous effort opened her swollen eyes, she saw no sign of flames. She stood up and lifted the little girl, then hurried to the window. But once there, she had to lay Bridget down on the floor. She needed both hands to open the window.

Out of a deep need to let the child know she hadn't been abandoned, Katie planted one heeled boot firmly on the skirt of Bridget's smoke-grimed, flowered dress. Maybe the little girl wouldn't know someone was there ... but maybe she would. Then, too, it was Katie's way of keeping track of the child, should the smoke thicken again.

Suddenly there were flames, small ones, dancing in and out of a tall bookcase standing against the wall opposite her, near the door. Like children playing hide-and-go-seek, Katie thought, even as the sense of urgency within her mushroomed. How long would it be before the infant flames, fed by the pages of the shelved books, grew up?

If she could get some air into her lungs, the constant coughing would stop, the sharp knives carving into her chest might go away, and then perhaps she could think straight.

Keeping her right heel firmly planted on Bridget's dress, Katie examined the window. The glass was smoke-grimed, but when she looked down, she could see the scene below. There in the street were two fire engines, parked helter-skelter. The crowd of neighbors and spectators had thickened to a deep, wide, puddle of people. Katie saw her uncle Malachy, still in his iron-gray work clothes. He was standing with his arm around Lottie. She must have telephoned him, summoning him home. Had Tom come, too? Katie didn't see him. Her aunt was openly crying and twisting in agitation the flowered apron tied around her waist. Behind her stood Flo, an anxious look on her face.

Someone saw her then, an elderly woman

Katie didn't recognize. The woman opened her mouth in a shout, and pointed. The firemen looked up, along with everyone else.

Spots were appearing in front of her eyes, blue, yellow, purple, dancing like the flames near the door. And the room had begun slowly spinning around her, like the wonderful carousel at Coney Island. But this kind of spinning was not so wonderful. Katie guessed that the spots meant she was close to passing out. She had never fainted in her life, not even when she broke her elbow. She dare not do it now. They would both perish for certain.

She reached out and undid the latch. It took every ounce of strength she had to raise the window. But it was worth the effort, as cold air smelling of smoke rushed into the room. Katie gulped it in gratefully, and at the same time, reached down to scoop up the unconscious child and lay her head on the windowsill, as close to the air as possible.

It took her only a second to realize the price she would pay for the fresh air. The incoming oxygen had fueled the baby flames, transforming them from playful little creatures to full-blown, adult flames, grasping like tentacles for everything in their path.

They had already, in just seconds, swallowed up the door.

There was no way out of the room.

# Chapter 22

Bridget hung from the windowsill, limp as a rag doll. From below came shouting. It was Katie's name they were shouting. And something else . . . "Jump! Jump, Katie!"

Jump? From the second story?

Then Mary's voice, surprisingly strong. "Did you find her, Katie? Did you find my Bridget? Is she all right, then?"

Other voices shouted, "Jump! You've got to jump!"

Katie looked down. There were five, no six firemen in black coats and helmets. Their extended arms supported a black cloth or canvas, round as pie. From where Katie stood, it looked no more substantial than a child's blanket. They weren't thinking, were they, that she was to jump into that? Or fling poor Bridget down upon it? Did they think the smoke had driven her daft? She turned away from the window, sagging against the windowframe. "Oh, Paddy, damn you," she whispered, "where *are* you? Why are you not here, as you were on the ship? Are you not goin' to save me this time, then?"

She knew he wasn't. He didn't even know she was in trouble. Such terrible trouble. And not just her. Bridget, too. Paddy liked Bridget. He would be sore distressed to see the child in such a state.

The flames had swallowed up a full quarter of the room. They consumed flowered wallpaper, a wall sconce, a wooden valet supporting a blue serge man's jacket, an inexpensive fake leather jewelry box and its contents, a floor lamp with a pink fringed shade, a pile of clean white pillowslips neatly folded on a brown wooden chair. Then they ate the chair. Katie watched in horror.

There was no more time.

"Jump!" came from below. "You must jump!"

She knew the voices were right. She felt again for Bridget's pulse. Still there . . . but oh, so faint. If there was any chance at all . . . Mary must have her child. She would never forgive herself if her baby died.

"Oh, Lord," Katie whispered, "you ask too much of me, and that's the truth of it. But I guess I got no choice. I'll do it then, if I must." Then she muttered grimly, "But I'm sayin' right now I won't *like* it!"

Turning back to the window, she hoisted Bridget up over the sill. When Mary glimpsed the red curls, she cried out in joy and shouted, "Bless you, Katie, bless you!"

Even with a voice, Katie wouldn't have had the heart to shout, "Don't bless me yet, Mary. You haven't seen the state your child is in." The only blessing was, as far as she could tell, Bridget wasn't burned. It was the smoke that had done her in, poisoning her little lungs. Looking at her pinched, gray-blue face and her limp body, it was impossible to believe that Mary's Bridget would ever walk, run, play, *breathe* normally again.

"I cannot toss this child out the window," Katie whispered to the gluttonous flames. "I cannot!"

But she did. Dropping the little girl out into space was the hardest thing Kathleen Hanrahan had ever had to do. Worse even than stepping off the great ship *Titanic* into a lifeboat. But now, as then, she had no choice.

The child landed softly, gently, just as Katie had hoped. One of the firemen scooped her up, cradling her in his arms, and rushed with her to a waiting ambulance. Mary and Agnes Murphy raced along behind him. Both climbed into the back of the ambulance before it pulled away, siren wailing.

Katie, her breath coming in agonizing, ragged gasps, fell to her knees. She knew she had only been inside the house ten minutes or less. It seemed days.

"Jump, Katie, jump!" her uncle Malachy shouted from below. "Hurry! Jump now!"

If only there were a lifeboat hanging on davits right outside the window, like the one she'd stepped into from the *Titanic*. She would step into it then and someone above her would slowly, safely, lower it down to the ground. She wouldn't even mind if it lurched like a drunken donkey, as the lifeboat had. As long as it got her out of this inferno and safely to the ground.

But there *was* no lifeboat here. The only way to the ground was a dive, a leap out into empty space. What if she missed the canvas? She would escape death by fire only to die of a broken neck or smashed skull.

If I'm ever goin' to see Paddy again, Katie thought as another wave of coughing overtook her, if I'm ever goin' to see Ireland again and me sisters and brother, me ma and da, I'm goin' to have to take a leap out this window and I'm goin' to have to be quick about it. She did so want to see Ireland again. Even if it meant boarding a ship.

Closing her red and swollen eyes, she pulled herself to her feet and climbed over the wooden sill until she was perched on it. Heat from the flames gobbling their way toward her seared the back of her neck. Terror made her oxygen-deprived heart skip, slow, skip again, as if it were trying to decide whether or not to go on with the struggle. Afraid it would give up before she could jump, Katie stared down at the black canvas circle just long enough to take aim. Then she leaned forward, took a deep breath, and closed her eyes.

"Jesus, Mary, and Joseph," she whispered, "I give you my heart and my soul."

Then she jumped.

# Chapter 23

Elizabeth had been staying with Anne, in her shockingly messy and postage stamp-sized apartment under the el, for only two days when there was a commanding knock at the door. Anne had gone out to hear her idol, Emma Goldman, a fiery, free-thinking speaker, give a speech in the Village. "You should come, too, Elizabeth, you'd be inspired," she had urged. But Elizabeth, desperately needing to be alone with her thoughts after two days and nights of Anne, declined.

Thinking it was Max at the door, Elizabeth hurried to answer it.

Nola was standing on the other side. Dressed in a chic navy blue suit with a white blouse, and a matching blue hat on her head, she looked thoroughly shaken. Elizabeth understood that when Nola left her house for Anne's apartment, she couldn't possibly have known what the neighborhood was really like. If she had, perhaps she would have stayed home.

"Where did you get this address?" Elizabeth asked.

"From Max. It wasn't easy. He really is terribly stubborn, Elizabeth. I can't see how you can find that attractive. Still, he did help me understand a few things. He isn't stupid, I'll grant that much."

Max had been after her to call her mother, straighten things out. Elizabeth knew he meant well, but she hadn't seen any point to that. A waste of time . . . still, here was her mother now, standing in front of her.

Without waiting for permission, Nola moved past Elizabeth, stopping in shock just inside the door. "Good heavens, Elizabeth, you can't possibly prefer *this* to your own home! Why, it's . . . it's . . ." Apparently unable to find a word in her vocabulary that suited Anne's shabby, messy apartment, Nola fell silent.

Elizabeth closed the door. "What do you want, Mother? Why are you here?"

Nola turned to face her daughter. "I want you to come home. Now. With me. Joseph is waiting downstairs."

"But I don't want to. You lied to me. You frightened me. I don't trust you anymore. I don't want to live with you." Ignoring Nola's wince, Elizabeth continued, "I've already spoken to a lovely woman at Vassar, in Admissions. They will allow me to begin classes in mid-January, and they'll reinstate my scholarship. I'll be living on campus, coming back to the city on weekends to see Max and my friends here. That's what I'm going to do, Mother. Until then, I'm staying here. Anne may be a radical, but she has a generous heart."

She moved over to stand at the window. It was filthy with grime, which she perversely hoped Nola noticed. The windows in the Farr house were always gleaming. "I suppose I should thank you. *And* Claire. If you hadn't done what you did, and Claire hadn't told me about it, I might never have left that house. And you would still be telling me what to do and where to go and how to dress and . . ."

"I won't do that anymore," Nola said in a small voice.

Elizabeth laughed. "Yes, you will. You can't help it." More seriously, she added, "What you and Dr. Cooper did was unforgivable."

Nola sighed heavily. She glanced about the room and, finding no uncluttered place to sit, joined Elizabeth at the window. "I don't know what Claire told you, but Fenton only does what he does for women who lost husbands . . . sons . . . on the *Titanic*. Women who are so terrified of being further abandoned, they really *are* sick. Heartsick. Frightened. They know what it's like to lose someone they loved, and they're frightened to death that it will happen again. So he gives them just this tiny heart condition. Is that so terrible? To make sure there will always be *someone* there for them."

"But it isn't true. It's a lie."

"It *is* true!" Nola's sudden passion startled Elizabeth. It was so unlike her mother. "It is *not* a lie! These are women whose hearts *are* troubled, all the time, every second, skipping beats every time they remember that night. And they remember it a *lot*. Skipping beats when they think about being even more alone than they already are because the daughter who survived when the son and husband did not is about to marry and move away, or go away to school, or leave for Europe with friends, or join the suffrage movement or take a job in an office building. Their hearts skip a beat when they think of having to spend a holiday all alone in a big house, with no one there to share it. These are hearts already damaged, if not broken completely in two, by what happened out on the sea. They can't take any more pain, and that, Elizabeth, *is* true. Fenton Cooper knows that, and he understands."

A train rumbled by overhead, making it impossible for Elizabeth to be heard. When it had passed, she said quietly, "I'm sorry, Mother. I guess I didn't realize . . . you all seemed fine after a while. All of the women. You all went shopping and to concerts and plays, and I thought you were all doing amazingly well. I'm sorry."

"That's just how we do things." Nola paused, then pleaded, "Elizabeth, if you'll just come home, I promise you things will change. I'll be different. You can go to Vassar and you can do as you please. I won't interfere."

"Mother . . ."

"I know you don't believe me. I don't blame you. But it's true."

Elizabeth decided Nola *did* mean it. Now. At this moment, in this place, her mother meant every word she was saying. But once back in the Murray Hill house, the old behavior would take over. Nola couldn't help it. The time would approach for Elizabeth to leave and if her mother didn't actually have an "episode," she'd come up with some other reason why Elizabeth should "wait a while" before leaving for Pough-keepsie. Perhaps she'd bring up her daughter's promise to her father. She would think of something. That was just who she was.

"I'm not coming home, Mother. I'm sorry. But . . ." Elizabeth saw her father's face as Max had painted him. Brave. Sad. But trusting as he gazed out upon the departing lifeboats that his wife and daughter would survive, would be all right, would go on with their lives when he could not go on with his. "But I will come to see you. Before I leave for Poughkeepsie. And when I come back to the city on weekends. Perhaps we could even go shopping once in a while. Not *every* weekend, though." She smiled. "I don't have the stamina that you have."

It was almost impossible for Nola to admit defeat. "But it's so much nicer at home. This place . . ." She glanced around again. "It's not very clean, is it? You could stay at home just until you leave for school."

"No, it's not very clean. But Anne doesn't mind. Nor do I, although," Elizabeth smiled, "I had thought about straightening up a bit while she's out." The finality in her voice was unmistakable.

A light died in Nola's eyes. Just as quickly, another appeared, proving her resilience. "You really will visit me on a weekend now and again? You're not just saying that so I'll leave now, are you?"

"Mother, I wouldn't lie about something like that. I meant it."

Nola's eyes filled with tears. "And you won't forget?"

"I won't forget. Why don't we make a date right now, while you're here? There's a calendar somewhere in all this mess." Elizabeth found the calendar, smeared with dried jelly and coffee stains. "There, the last weekend in

January, why not then? That will give me two weeks to get settled on campus. I'll telephone you and let you know how things are going, and we can make plans." But," she warned, "*no* dinners at the Winslows, can we agree on that?"

Nola said with a straight face, "Oh, but they're so fond of *you*. Especially Betsy."

Elizabeth smiled. "Promise me, Mother."

Nola nodded. "I promise. All right then, the last weekend in January. I shall look forward to it. And perhaps," she said, turning toward the door, "next summer when there are no classes, you might think about joining me in Atlantic City. Max could go with Jules and Enid and then we'd all be there together, wouldn't that be fun, dear?"

Elizabeth smiled. That was Nola, trying to sweeten the pot by tossing in Max, when not so long ago she hadn't wanted him anywhere in sight. "I may look for a job next summer, Mother. For the experience. But we'll see. Atlantic City is always fun. We can talk about it later. Now I really should clean up around here a bit before Anne gets back."

Nola took the hint. Though she was hurt and probably, if the truth were known, angry that she hadn't accomplished what she'd come there to do, she did give Elizabeth a hug. The hug, Elizabeth knew, was a way for Nola to pretend she'd gained more ground than she actually had. But that was all right. Elizabeth wanted the hug, too.

She stood in the doorway watching her elegantly dressed mother cautiously descend the shabby wooden steps, glancing around her the whole time, as if afraid a thief might at any moment jump out and snatch her purse out of her hands. Nola Farr in a shabby building under the el . . . now there was a sight Max would never paint. He'd shrug and say, "Who would believe it?"

That night, she related to him, in careful detail, every moment of her mother's astonishing visit. "You helped," she said when she had finished. "I don't know what you said to her, she didn't tell me. But it made a difference. She didn't argue half as long as she usually does."

"I wasn't rough on her, if you're worried about that." They were in his apartment, alone, on his old davenport, Elizabeth in his arms, leaning against his chest. "I guess I would have been, before the unveiling. But that business about the paintings, I guess it showed me how differently everyone has dealt with what happened out there on the ocean. Everyone grieves in a different way, seems to me. Maybe that's why people have such a hard time talking about it. We're all thinking differently. No common ground, though you'd think that's exactly what we have, since we were all *there*. We all went through it. But we reacted differently." He looked down at Elizabeth, comfortably nestled in his arms. "Are you worried that you've broken your promise to your father?"

"No. Because he was wrong about my mother. He thought she needed taking care of, because that's how their marriage was. And it worked, for them. But it isn't true. Whether she marries again or not, she can take care of herself. I believe that. She said as much herself, at Alan's. And I think as long as I don't shut her out of my life completely, which I don't intend to do, she'll be fine."

Max sat up straight and fished something out of his jacket pocket. "Speaking of marriage . . ." He held out a small, navy blue velvet box. "This was my grandmother's. She left it to me." He opened the box, revealing a simple but beautiful solitaire diamond set in a gold band. "I want you to marry me, Elizabeth. We can get a better apartment, if you want. I have my grandmother's money. And you can still go to Vassar, still do all the things you want. A weekend marriage is fine with me, for now. Will you?"

Elizabeth took the box from him. "Oh, Max, it's beautiful! I love it. But . . . but marriage? Now?" She loved Max with all her heart. She couldn't have made it through these past months without him. But it had taken her so long to work up enough courage to leave her mother's house, to be on her own, to make her own life. She would hardly be on her own if she married Max. She would have a husband. No wife she had ever met could be considered "on her own," though she supposed there were those who were more independent. The women who marched for the vote, who spoke at rallies . . . some of them must be married. But not knowing any of them personally, she couldn't say how their marriages were.

Max looked hurt, and disappointed. "You don't want to marry me?"

"Yes, of course I do." She couldn't bear the thought of hurting him. "It's just . . . well, could we be engaged now but wait a while to marry? Would that be all right? I love you so much, Max, but I know I'm not ready to be married. Could I just be a student first? There is so much I need to learn before I can be a wife."

He looked uncertain. "What if you meet someone else up in Poughkeepsie? Someone you like better?"

"Better than *you*?" Elizabeth laughed softly. "Oh, Max, don't be silly! There *isn't* anyone I could like better than you . . . *love* better than you. There just isn't." She took the ring from its box and put it on her left hand. Then she lifted his hand and put it to her cheek. "I promise," she said solemnly, "that I will marry you. If you will promise to wait until I'm ready."

With the ring on her finger, Max seemed to relax, just a bit. "I promise, though I can't say I'm happy about it. How do I know you won't change your mind? You might become one of those women your mother's always going on about, the ones who have no use for men. You could decide never to marry anyone."

"Oh, I couldn't do that," Elizabeth said seriously. "I have to marry. I'm sure I will need furniture moved one day."

Max, who was familiar with all of Anne's sayings, threw his head back and laughed.

Then, to seal their engagement, he kissed Elizabeth thoroughly.

# Chapter 24

It was Mary who called Paddy on Christmas Eve to tell him Katie was in the hospital. "'Tis her I'm owin'," she said with tears in her voice. "She saved me only child, she did, and she needs to see you, Paddy. It ain't John she wants, it's you. She don't know I'm callin'. You'd best get yourself out here to the hospital quick as a wink. But," she added quickly, "she can't talk. You can't be expectin' her to. Her voice is gone. Not for all time, the doctors say, but for now. The smoke . . . still and all, *you* can talk to *her*." Mary's voice hardened. "You can tell her how sorry it is you are for bein' faithless with that Belle person, takin' her to Coney Island when you knew full well Katie thought of it as your special place." She explained then that Katie had been there that night, too, had seen Paddy with Belle, how heart-broken she had been. "Still is, if you ask me."

He was in Katie's hospital ward within the hour. Looking disheveled from the rush, carrying a brown paper bag in his hands, he burst into the long, narrow room filled with white beds and waved Lottie and Malachy, sitting beside Katie's bed, away. "She can't talk," Lottie warned as they left. "Don't be arguin' with her."

He had no intention of arguing with her. He dropped into a chair and took both of her hands in his. She looked terrible. Her eyes were swollen and red-rimmed, her skin grayish. One arm was bandaged above the elbow. "Are you all right, then?" he asked. According to Mary's account of the fire, he could just as easily have been looking at a corpse. The thought made him sick. He couldn't have stood it, had she died in that house. "We need to be talkin', Katie. I know you're not feelin' well, but we got to get some things straight."

She shook her head, touching her throat.

"I know. You can't talk. Mary told me." He dumped the contents of the brown paper bag on the white sheet covering Katie. Wooden alphabet blocks, twenty-six of them, the letters painted in white on all sides but one, on which there was a drawing of an animal or a toy. "I stopped at Mary's on the way here ... they're stayin' with Lottie and Malachy until

Agnes's house is fixed up ... and borrowed these. Bridget's here, too, in the kiddies' ward, and doin' fine, Mary says. She won't be missin' these until she goes home. Lottie said I could use them." Paddy leaned closer to Katie. "I need to ask you some questions, Katie-girl, need to in the worst way. I was thinkin', you could use the blocks to answer, if you're feelin' up to it. Are you?"

She nodded.

"All right, then." He lined up the blocks on her sheet, four uneven rows of them, wobbling slightly but their letters clearly visible. "Here's the first question. Do you hate me, then?"

Katie lifted her uninjured arm to point. **NO**

"And is it John Donnelly you're wantin' in your life now?"

**NO**

He heaved a sigh of relief. Taking her hands in his again, he said, "Mary was tellin' me you saw me with Belle at Coney Island. We was only talkin' about the writin'. Her beau came along with us. He was there, too. You must have come upon us when he was off finding somethin' for us to eat." He shook his head. "Why did you not tell me? You could have telephoned, told me what you was thinkin'. I'd have told you the truth. So that's my next question. Why didn't you tell me what you was thinkin'?"

The hand moved again. It pained Paddy that it moved so slowly, that Katie had so little strength. **STUBBORN**

Paddy smiled. "You?" he asked. "Or me?"

**BOTH**

"Aye, that's the truth. I could have come to talk to you, find out for myself why you wasn't talkin' to me, and I didn't. It was 'cause I thought you was better off without me, you doin' so well and all."

She shook her head and pointed. **NOT WELL**

Nodding, Paddy said, "Well, I know you're not well now. But that's because of the fire. You was incredible brave, Katie. Everyone says so. Like Bri. He was that brave, too. You'd have made a fine pair, the two of you."

**STOP THAT**

"Stop what?"

The finger pointed quickly, moving rapidly from one block to another in exasperation. **BRIAN GONE SORRY MISS HIM BUT LOVE YOU BRIAN HAPPY FOR US**

Paddy's expression was bleak. "I think about him, Katie. I try not to, but the thoughts come. They're terrible thoughts, me up here, alive, him on the bottom of the ocean. . . ."

Katie reached up to put a finger to Paddy's lips. She mouthed, "Shh!" Then she pointed again. **DONT BE DUMB BRIAN NOT THERE IN OCEAN YOU KNOW BETTER PADDY**

"But I *see* him there, plain as day!"

She pointed again, this time tapping each block with such force several tipped over. **NOT THERE HE IS IN WARM SAFE GOOD PLACE YOU KNOW THAT SAY IT PADDY SAY THATS WHERE BRIAN IS NOW**

He looked dubious, but Katie could see he was trying, that he wanted to believe her.

**STUBBORN BRI SAFE HAPPY YOU KNOW TRUE**

At last he nodded. Tears of relief appeared in his eyes. "You're right. He's not there. I shouldn't have been thinkin' it all this time. It was wrong thinkin' on my part." His voice almost a whisper, he said, "It came from me not understandin' why I lived and he didn't. It's tearin' me to pieces, Katie, wonderin' that."

The tears that filled her swollen eyes then were angry ones. Her jabs were rapid and furious, as if the blocks themselves had offended her. **IT DONT MATTER WHY YOU JUST LIVED THATS ALL NOW YOU GOT TO DO SOMETHING WE WASNT SAVED FROM TITANIC TO DO NOTHING PADDY DO IT FOR BRIAN FOR ME FOR YOU ITS TIME**

"You mean the book."

**YES**

Paddy thought about that. Mary had said it was a wonder that Katie had lived, that everyone was certain she would die in that house. But she hadn't. Maybe because he needed her so. And maybe *he* hadn't died on the *Titanic* along with Brian because *he* was needed. It wouldn't hurt to think so. "Will you help? I mean, I know you're busy and all, singin', but . . ."

She touched her throat again.

"Oh, I know, but Mary says you'll sing again. Not for a while, though. Maybe you could help me get goin' on the book till then? When you're feelin' better, I mean. And then when you're singin' again, I promise I'll come. 'Twas pigheaded of me not to. If you want me to, that is."

**I WANT AND I WANT IRELAND SOME-DAY**

Paddy nodded. "I been thinkin' on that. I guess I'd like to see my ma and da again. And granda. I should be tellin' them how brave Bri was. They'd like knowin' that."

**YOU MEAN IT**

"Yes, I mean it. Some day. If the book sells and there's money enough. I mean it."

**PROMISE**

"I promise." Paddy bent to kiss Katie's aching throat.

She reached down and gently tugged on his hair to lift his head up. Then she began tapping the blocks again. **SING PROMISE**

Paddy laughed. "Are you daft? You're the singer, not me."

**PLEASE SING IT**

He was so glad she was alive, that she hadn't died, not only on the *Titanic*, but again in Agnes Murphy's roominghouse. The months without her had been miserable and he had not expected them to end. He had thought to go on forever without her. The thought had brought a constant ache to his chest. Now, he would do anything to prove that he never intended to let her go again. He would even sing, if that was what it took.

"You'll be regrettin' this," he said, "as will everyone else in this ward." But then he sat back in the chair, still holding Katie's hands, and he lifted his head and began to sing in a clear Irish tenor, "I'll take you home again, Kathleen..."

Katie closed her eyes. But she was smiling.

# Epilogue

They had come together once again, two years after the tragedy, to gather at the Seamen's Church Institute in New York City. In some faces the pain had eased a bit, in others it was still as fresh and raw as it had ever been.

Holding tightly to Paddy's hand, Katie gazed up at the Memorial Lighthouse and thought of Brian. She had meant what she said to Paddy. Brian was not in the ocean, he couldn't be. She was just as certain that in the warm, safe refuge he had found, he was pleased that his brother was here now, with her, that they were still together and always would be. He would understand how Paddy still struggled with his book, but be proud that he hadn't given up, that he kept trying. Paddy would finish the book one day, and they would both thank Edmund Tyree for his patience, and Belle for all her help.

She hadn't given up hope of one day getting

her voice back. The doctors Paddy took her to were encouraging. He teased her, saying he liked her hoarse, dry whispering. But she sorely missed the singing. Flo had been so kind, bringing flowers and magazines to Lottie's house, sometimes small toys for Bridget, who was healthy and active again. Flo had never once said, "Didn't I tell you the smoke would ruin your voice?" She was a good woman.

Paddy hadn't forgotten his promise to take her back to Ireland. He mentioned it every once in a while. When he was in a really good mood, he even sang the song for her again. They would need money for the trip, and more important, the courage to board a ship again.

Once there, they might stay, they might not. Did it really matter? They were alive when she, at least, might not have been, and they were together. It wasn't the place that mattered. It was, Katie had decided, who was with you, wherever you were, that mattered.

Elizabeth felt a measure of peace for the first time since she'd begun attending the memorial services honoring her father and so many others lost on the *Titanic*. Last year at this time, her dreams had seemed to disappear along with the ship itself. Now, at last, she was beginning to fulfill them. She loved college. It was everything she had hoped it would be. Max was painting well . . . she'd seen some of his new work, wonderfully detailed New York scenes that she felt certain would draw positive attention. Her mother, while never ceasing to complain that she saw too little of her daughter, was at least civil to Max now. That was progress.

They still had a long way to go. But they had managed to survive a monumental disaster at sea and, almost more difficult, they had survived two years of grief and adjustment. Elizabeth wasn't sure how, exactly. There had been many times when she had doubted they would manage. But they had.

Max said occasionally, "We've been through the worst. It can only get better from here on in."

Perhaps he was right.

*"Those we loved and lost..."* a speaker's voice broke into her thoughts.

No one spoke then as the ball in the *Titanic* Memorial Lighthouse mounted on the rooftop of the Seamen's Church Institute in New York City dropped once again, in memory of fifteen hundred people lost at sea.